About the Author

The author has experience in building conservation work and has a passion for, and discovering, hidden history.

The Siege Machine

Walter C Roberts

The Siege Machine

Olympia Publishers
London

www.olympiapublishers.com
OLYMPIA PAPERBACK EDITION

A CIP catalogue record for this title is
available from the British Library.

ISBN: 978-1-78830-940-0

First Published in 2021

Olympia Publishers
Tallis House
2 Tallis Street
London
EC4Y 0AB
Printed in Great Britain

Dedication

Hayley

CHAPTER 1
CRY CITY

Sidney Picket surfaced from a deep, long sleep, to the chirping of house sparrows, their fluttering noisy squabbling came from the eaves of a dormer window by his bed. These comforting sounds fade as the memory of his disturbing discovery returned, he wanted to resist and sink back into blissful slumber, but chilling apprehension took hold—things were not as they should be.

Sidney's one bedroom flat occupied the roof space of a large, tired looking, four storey Georgian house overlooking the river. He had been there for three years, and each spring promised himself he would move the bed, but he never did, he knew he would regret it; he loved sparrows, they had become family. In any event, he had a big day ahead and was grateful for the early morning call, it was 7.20 p.m. and the stirrings of Cry City would grow as the sun rose. Sidney dressed carefully, he preferred starting the day neat and fresh. He decided to immerse himself in menial domestic tasks, to keep his mind from dwelling on his suspicions; he needed to stay focussed for today's event, distractions would not be helpful.

Battle-Cry Castle, as the name would suggest, has a bloody and chequered history. Its prominent position on the edge of the River Cry, attracted over the centuries many fierce and ferocious battles. Its ravaged stone battlements, castle keep, and towers pay tribute to the durability of its fabric and the medieval workmen who raised it in 1089. Its battlements overlooking the river soared up some thirty metres from the river level and presented a formidable challenge for attacking ships. Cry bridge would be the first obstacle, as they sailed up with the tide from the sea. The Cry City outer wall was another bastion, but sadly no more, years of neglect, lack of usefulness and a need for valuable building material sealed its fate. The castle did not fare much better, it was left roofless. Sidney had been told that the name for the city had originated from an ancient member of the Guild of Town Cryers, and that the voice of the officiating cryer, one Jackob Job, was so powerful, his cry could be heard over a mile away. It was a tale his grandfather had often told him, but Sidney knew it was a tall one. The theologians have a more rational explanation. At a time when Christianity was in turmoil, with Rome, monks, and the reformation, certain sections of the faith decided to call themselves: crypto Christians. That is those Christians, who, in order to avoid persecution, hide their faith—cry wolf!

Sidney had lived in the City of Cry all his life, apart from a stint in university and a year travelling the globe. Cry was his home, his roots and where his heart was. It was this emotional connection that made him sensitive to the situation he found himself in. He was fearful that the people he was involved with would change things, possibly change his life, and not for the good. Walking along the promenade, heading towards the High Street, he reflected on the medieval structure at the right hand side of the road. The imposing rugged stone castle, its battlements soaring up into the air, it was something built for war, but what's new? He was in a war now, and at a loss to know how to deal with it—a war of manipulation and secrecy.

Within a stone's throw of the keep and built at the same time is Cry church, Norman, but with Anglo Saxon origins, later remodelling gave the façade an austere, but dignified look. It is, but not in name, a cathedral. It has the look and bearing of one but has been demoted in status by man—but not by God! The Normans, with fierce continental gospel fervour, had invaded and conquered Britain, and Cry church, the city's spiritual house, was their legacy of endeavour. Sidney did attend services from time to time but preferred the local chapel his parents had attended. Sadly, they had completed their stay on Earth. Sidney's journey to heaven however, was a rebellious one, full of questions and doubts and his biggest gripe, why should there be wars?

It was Sidney's place of birth. The medieval City of Cry nestles under the brooding presence of the towering castle keep with many fragments of a high outer city wall. These fragments are interspersed with Victorian encrustations and gaps, which are filled with modern architecture of dubious taste. The ancient High Street has been subjected to alterations and additions over the years, but its historic heart was largely intact and joins with the bridge on the River Cry. To be more precise: bridges, for there are three: one in stone: one in concrete: and one in steel. From his lofty abode, mainly through the bathroom window, Sidney has a glimpse of the older bridge and the embankment running south, it was a peaceful sight, but peace was not what he was feeling at this moment.

Suspicion, it was not a word that Sidney was comfortable with. He was trusting, not suspicious by nature and found those that were—odd. To suspect that under every stone a serpent would be found, would only induce timidity and fear, that was his simple outlook. But suspicion had come, nagging at first, a subtle, vague feeling that something was wrong. This had turned recently into a real awareness that something was seriously wrong, but who could he confide in, certainly not his boss.

The project Sidney was working on in the architects' studio was challenging. On the one hand, innovative and exciting, but on the other hand—weird, there was no other word for it. It was the client. A Peruvian based company called, 'Goth Enactment's'; presumably they thought a touch of the European would help. The Peruvian operatives in England were difficult to work with and communications were sometimes near impossible. Sidney felt that was intentional, also, their level of secrecy was disturbing, and he hated to admit it—suspicious. He had slept badly and had a quick shower, but this did nothing to dispel his troubled thoughts.

To Sidney's eye, the stone bridge over the river, the earliest and Victorian, was the most attractive of the three bridges. The quality of the workmanship, a reflection of the era, gave it a dignified look. The concrete bridge is a 1960s' innovation: cost being the driving force, culminating in the bridge having a strong utilitarian appearance. The steel bridge was designed for trains and has an abundance of steel lattice framing, that constantly needed painting, he had always thought the colour coordination could be improved. No signs of the earlier medieval bridge exist.

Sidney's flat was a ten-minute walk from the studio where he worked, and opposite it a small, but tasteful cosmopolitan café just off the High Street. He sipped his americano and meditated on the looming presentation ahead. The day was going to be eventful; he had all his drawings ready, on his laptop and hard copies. He would normally be nervous at presentations, but his suspicions had hardened his attitude and he felt oddly aggressive, but in a positive way, he felt it gave him an edge—he would need something extra for today's meeting.

The River Cry was a half mile wide ribbon of olive green-brown water, when on the ebb, as the sea tide merged with the muddy fresh flood water. And when wind over tide; a tumultuous grey-green-blue. Sidney loved its changing moods. He had seen many old photos and often wondered how it would have been in medieval times? Cry once a place of commerce and trading ships, now all gone, a barren river and port, as though nature was claiming it back—flotsam, jetsam and oil slicks a thing of the past.

The City of Cry is not a sleepy place, the hustle and bustle of its many inhabitants an echo of its ancient history—there is a great propensity for re-enactments. There are occasions when people dress up and walk about, some strolling elegantly, some slowly slouching beggar like, and others giggling girlishly and ghoulishly. It comes alive with swarming, jostling, gentle folk. Car parking arrangements are obliterated by this mass of humanity bent on enjoyment; often artificial snow would be created for seasonal effect. Sidney wasn't too keen on this foreign intrusion and tended to drift away, these gay, noisy occasions, had lost their novelty.

Deep within this honeycombed City of Cry, Sidney Picket lived and worked, a young man with hopes and aspirations, a young man whose destiny was about to be revealed. An assistant of longstanding to Herbert Strange, an eccentric architect and sole practitioner. Sidney was following in his master's footsteps and loved the conservation work, the architect's speciality. Odd though Herbie was, Sidney admired him in many ways. He was bold, impetuous and totally without self-consciousness and being with him at one of his presentations was a challenge, to Sidney's own self-consciousness and to all those present. Herbie would do and say things that would cause much embarrassment and discomfort. "Shock and awe." he would exclaim. "Shock and awe, my boy, that's what they need." He was always kindly towards Sidney though, but then Sidney did do most of the work.

All agreed that met him, Sidney was a polite young man, well-mannered and groomed to perfection, fastidiously so, one might say. But underneath this well-manicured, gentlemanly exterior was a steely personality, his mother said, he followed in his father's footsteps, once he set his mind on a thing, he would never let go. It was this stubbornness that Herbie exploited, he could always rely on the quality of Sidney's work and he always finished the job. Sidney was aware of everyone's perception of him, he had gone to great lengths to cultivate it. It was a defence mechanism, he disliked criticism and tried to avoid confrontations, but usually won when challenged. Working for Herbie, with all his foibles, helped control his own streak of stubbornness.

Sidney sat at the window of the café. Dan the waiter brought over his coffee and toast. "Todays the big day then Sid." He was a dapper man with a winning smile. "Old Herbie would be lost without you, he as good as said so the other day; I reckon you should ask for more money." He wandered back to the counter leaving Sidney to dream of the benefits that would bring, and should he ask? Herbie was notoriously mean and took great offence when pressed on matters relating to money. Sidney had to admit, his salary was poor, but there were benefits, he was given a free hand. Herbie liked to proclaim the vision and leave the detail to Sidney, an arrangement that suited them both.

Stubborn though Sidney was, he also had a strong tendency to please. This subservient inclination was further enhanced, by his quiet, polite manner. In contrast to Herbie, who blustered his way through life and bullying his way through any challenges that were set before him—quiet and polite he certainly was not.

For all Herbies talents and attributes, he had one major flaw in his intellectual reasoning, he couldn't understand drawings. Now this impediment had a negative effect on his progress in the early years until the advent of Computer Aided Design, this technology had come to his rescue just in time. Sidney produced the drawings on the computer and Herbie did all the talking. He never did grasp the principals of reading drawings and relied on Sidney to produce 3D images on his computer. But even then, he wasn't fully grasping it and Sidney ended up making physical models of his various projects, whether the client wanted one made or not. It was a task that Sidney enjoyed, in fact it was one the reasons he stayed with Herbie, job satisfaction. This latest model, now ready for the presentation, would be the pinnacle of Sidney's short, but active career. It was a scaled model, in wood, of the proposed medieval Siege Machine, a heavily built, fortified structure on wheels designed to storm castles.

There is another place of special significance in the City of Cry and that is the Guild Hall. A meeting place for Master Craftsman. Sidney a fourth-generation Picket; his Great-great-grandfather was a shipbuilder and builder of local fishing smacks. Thirty-five footers, built for fishing the estuaries, a trade now long gone, but probably the reason for his keenness to build the medieval wooden machine. To be proud of a past you have never experienced was difficult for Sidney, but he did appreciate the values. He could see the Guild Hall clock, time for work, he had a lot of preparation ahead. He finished his coffee.

The common folk address the local authority as: That Crying City Council, when the official term is; "The City Upon-Cry Council", some use the spurious words, Prying or Trying City Council, this sarcasm did not go unnoticed and at times gained significant sympathetic support and amusement.

Sidney and his boss would be visiting Cry City Council offices later that day, which in stark contrast to the historic city it officiates over, is a large elongated dark red brick building of modern design. The several floor levels stepped back and up from the river's edge, following the lands natural rising contours, the entrance is from the higher, rear road level. It was given an award when its visual impact on the city was fully appreciated; it was a contentious decision. For some of the city dwellers, who possess an untrained eye, it appears to be a place of foreboding and bland indifference. For others who are more discerning and know its inner workings, it is a place of much mystery and excitement and like the castle, it sits on the banks of the River Cry. It is said, by Sidney's boss, that this award-winning office block has the appearance of a giant tree-fungus, protruding in layers and cascading down to the river's edge, with human spores floating in and out; and like all fungus, it will have a short life span, that was Herbies view. Sidney thought his boss was miffed at not getting the commission— jealousy brings the worst out in people.

The evening before, as Sidney reflected on the coming meeting and looking out at the council offices from his dormer window, his fertile imagination took over. To him this spreading organic growth on the edge of the river, as Herbie put it, took on another form. It had the eerie appearance of a multi-layered spacecraft. The shimmering reflections of the many lights in the water below, gave the impression it was gently landing. A thing that was alien, come to conquer and rule. A place of inhuman intelligence, a place of unlimited power, and he was going there tomorrow!

Deep within this complex organic structure that contains a myriad of working cells, lies a chamber. It is an inner sanctum, a place where the lives of people are changed forever; for good or for bad. It is the council chamber. A place where the planning committee meets, and decisions are made. Some wags call it the 'Crying Chamber', and for Herbie it would be a crying shame if his application was refused.

The tomorrow had come, today was the day. It was June and the temperature mid-twenties; and the chamber temperature was about to get hot. Very hot indeed. The committee sitting was about to decide whether to grant planning permission for a highly controversial project. It would be a decision that would affect many lives. Everything was ready, everyone was prepared, and Sidney, with a singular lack of faith, nervously hoped and prayed he was.

Herbert Strange, or Herbie as he was known to most, though not to his face, only his mother called him that. Was, to all who were convinced by him, to be a gifted conservation architect. He had been commissioned to prepare the scheme and it was requested by head of planning, and agreed, that he would make a formal presentation to the committee with his trusted assistant Sidney in attendance.

CHAPTER 2
THE CASE OFFICER

Penelope Pride was the planning officer assigned to the Siege Machine application. As case officer it was her duty to ensure that all the relevant facts were available for public inspection. It was the public consultation that Penelope disliked the most, verbal abuse from belligerent residents and the like seemed to get worse by the month; she said to her colleagues that society was in the process of disintegration. She had a cool, ice maiden look, but her beauty attracted venomous comments from female members of the public, but only from those that came with a grievance and needed personal counselling, rather than planning consolation. She had always taken the view that to be a good planner, a degree in psychology was essential—sadly she didn't have one.

She was getting ready for the big day and choosing her clothes with care, she didn't want to appear dowdy in front of Sidney, but the female members of the planning committee frowned upon over dressed women and she needed to take heed of their sensitivities. She was aware that she had a nice figure and could put on a decent show, but it was the level of femininity that was the issue. She decided to dress like a lawyer, a tailored suit, but with a bright floral shirt and cravat, a touch of lip gloss and leaving her long flaxen hair to flow down over her back. Satisfied that she had done her best for Sidney Picket, she went downstairs.

She sat at the kitchen table; her mother had made her a cup of tea. "You were up late last night my girl; you need your rest. I suppose it's that job of yours." She fussed at the sink. Penelope murmured a grateful acknowledgement; her mind was on Sidney; it was a relief her report was finished and ready for the meeting.

The application was unusual in many ways and attracted a lot of public interest. She couldn't imagine verbal abuse being attracted by this one, but you could never tell, the public were ever alert and looking for a chink, and Herbert Strange did tend to attract abuse. She was more than pleased that Sidney Picket was involved, he was sensible, attractive and dressed well. Although his boss did all the talking, she thought Sidney was the clever one. At previous consultation meetings she had seen him staring at her, she wondered if he liked her, she hoped so.

Penelope pondered over the visual impact the Siege Machine would have on Cry Castle. Using authentic warfare techniques would be challenging, but the benefits could be tremendous. Having worked for Cry City Council for five years, her rise in the ranks to case officer was meteoric, she had worked hard, and Nick Tweed, head of planning, liked her style. She had heard that he had said, she was a people's person, which was gratifying.

This unusual application had the office buzzing and she felt privileged that Nick trusted her to deal with Herbert Strange, who it must be said was strange by name and strange by nature. But with her soft attractive demeanour, Penelope got along with most people, including Herbie, who liked women. But then she liked Sidney, and that was the impetus she needed to put her shoulder to the wheel or wheels. To give planning permission for something that moved along a track and lobbed stones, was going to be interesting.

As she was musing over these issues, Bess, the family dog muzzled her arm, but sensing that her mistress was not ready for play sat back and waited, watching intently. Penelope wished she could change places with Bess right now, no meeting, no stress, no facing the committee, no job—just food and walkies—what bliss.

Sitting in her office in the Cry City Council building, Penelope was enmeshed in all the reports, the environmental impact being the most sensitive, she found herself, yet again, puzzling over certain aspects of Herbie's method statement. It was a document that he had prepared in support of the application. He constantly referred to the arc of the slinging arm of the Siege Machine; its length, some twenty metres and the weights needed to sling a missile. Which he went to great lengths to explain, would be a balloon filled with helium gas and a little water as weight to help it on its way. Too much water and spectators could get wet, too little and it would float up and away into the sky. Herbie said Sidney knew what he was doing and would give a demo if necessary. Penelope had complete confidence in Sidney but felt Herbie to be a bit woolly at times, he lacked attention to detail. However, his method statement was reasonable and supported by an engineer's report, putting emphasis on the six-degree sideways swivel movement of the throwing arm and the straightforward movement of the main structure on the ramp and its stability when being used. Vibration caused by the impact of the sling in action must be kept to a minimum. She was glad an engineer would be responsible for this one.

But there was another battle that Penelope needed to

face—the planning committee. It was going to be a challenging planning meeting. By some peculiar quirk of nature all the committee members had the same sense of humour, unfortunately it was not a bubbling good-natured sense of humour, but more of a warped sarcastic type with a spattering of cutting innuendoes. Penelope had always considered this a defence mechanism against interruption by spectators. Conducting themselves in the public eye was very much like acting and the committee room was their stage. But mercifully the humour was only conducted and directed at and between themselves. To ridicule the visiting public was considered bad form and Penelope, being a guest, was not expected to join in the repartee.

Nevertheless, it was always a daunting experience and certainly not wise to smirk or smile at the silliness of it. Many times, in the past she had the urge to giggle in the middle of the proceedings but managed to suppress it in time. The controlling strength of the chairperson's personality was the glue that held them all together, like the conductor of an out of tune band, but with everyone a keen trumpet player.

Her mobile phone buzzed; it was her boss, Nick Tweed. "Just checking, Penny, can you be a little early for the meeting tonight, I have a couple of tactical things I need to talk to you about." His voice sounded friendly enough, but she sensed he was anxious about the meeting; it was a contentious application.

"I can be there as early as you want; I have everything ready," she replied, trying to sound positive. As head of planning and conducting the meeting she assumed that he wanted things ready.

"That's great, shall we say four thirty p.m. in the reception area." There is something to be said in favour of a light-hearted committee, Penny thought, albeit based on sarcasm. But they did get things done, not perhaps to everyone's taste it must be said, but its results that count. Penelope sensed the pressure her boss was being put under, but his professionalism in dealing with the eccentric and volatile committee was commendable.

CHAPTER 3
THE MODEL

Herbert Strange, with his trusty pit prop Sidney Picket, arrived at the council offices early. Herbie, who was prone to panic, had formulated a plan: the presentation *must* go perfectly—there was a lot at stake, notwithstanding his fees. The biggest problem was the size of the model he had got Sidney to make for the project. It was 3.5 metres high when assembled and each of the elements making up the model needed to be carried lengthways to pass through various door openings, on its journey to the council chamber. It was not going to be easy. In fact, Sidney thought it a logistical nightmare, for his own personal reasons, but did not voice them: that would mean Herbie sulking and now was not the time for that. Sidney had cleared the whole process with the health and safety officer, who was reticent at first, wanting to bring in a moving contractor to do the work, but Sidney convinced him of the importance of secrecy that Herbie placed on the project, and he relented, but reluctantly.

The main reception of Cry City Council offices, with its muted green colours and display of royal flags, had a military atmosphere. The three doll-like receptionists, by subliminal agreement, responded to this and wore their hair as though they were in a Second World War enactment. Their faces set like granite with brightly painted lips, did not encourage the public to dawdle. To complete this formal, but cold hostile atmosphere, the reception interrogators sat behind a full height glazed screen, which was tinted dark grey at the top and graduating down to clear at eye level. Spattered all over this simulation of a night sky, were countless stars and constellations. One of the councillors was a keen amateur astrologer. The stars twinkled continuously when the screen was first installed, but members of the public were getting giddy looking up at it and a couple of children were physically sick, so the twinkling had to stop.

The model was in three sections and narrow enough to get through double doors and there were six sets of double doors all the way to the chamber, which was two levels below. Sidney always felt uncomfortable, it was as though they were entering the shaft of a Pyramid. The challenge was the 3.5-metre dimension. Herbie had agonised for weeks, revisiting and measuring numerous times, including the stairs, the goods lift was not big enough—today was the acid test.

Staggering, red faced and breathing heavily, Herbie carried the model with Sidney down the long wide footpath to the main entrance. Herbie's expensive Harris Tweed suit, already under pressure from his ample midriff, was now being tested to the limit! It would be practical to undo the buttons of his Scottish tartan waistcoat, but vanity disallowed; dignity and image were more important. His most treasured item of clothing: a yellow bow tie with red dots was now skew-whiff as he heaved and struggled with his precious cargo. Sweat was appearing on his brow and his cultivated mousy tousled hair was now damp, lank and sticking to his forehead.

Sidney a willowy, but muscular young man, who had the stature and grace of a Gazelle was now bending under the enormous weight. As usual, Sidney ended up carrying the heavy end. For Herbie, though extremely tall, was somewhat narrow in the shoulders, and in consequence lacked strength in his arms.

Sidney would have preferred some helping hands, but

Herbie was insisting on complete secrecy. Sidney, who had never worked on a project of this nature before and had been asked by Herbie to swear an oath of secrecy, formally, with a solicitor, he said it was the client's idea. Herbie was acting like a spy who had just come in from the cold. This furtive behaviour, to Sidney's mind, only made matters worse, panic was brewing. Far better a more casual approach, bearing in mind the application details were public knowledge anyway. His suspicions were growing about the client, but best not say anything to Herbie, he sensed he was in a delicate and unstable state of mind. Maybe it was the client's odd behaviour that was driving Herbie to react this way.

They made their way, slowly, painfully, towards the multi-accessed entrance of the council offices. The section of the model, the first, was covered with a white shroud giving their heavy burden the distinct appearance of an enormous coffin. Sidney was embarrassed, but Herbie insisted, he wanted a sense of mystery, it was paramount for his plan and the more macabre the better. Sidney was beginning to think they should be in medieval dress but was too physically and mentally stressed to care either way.

They staggered along the corridor, with a painfully slow, shuffling gait, more like a tortoise approaching a leaf sideways: Herbie stopped abruptly. He rested his end on the path, but insisted that Sidney, whose face was now an orange-red and his eyes bulging; to maintain holding his end up. But with a long agonising sigh Sidney lowered his end to the ground, Herbie gave him his best piercing look, but said nothing.

Which door should they use? With Herbie no action was ever taken without an in-depth discussion, usually with himself. Sidney would always wait patiently for his mentor and master to conclude. He told himself it was good self-discipline to do so.

"Obviously, we cannot go through the revolving doors." Herbie looked serious, "The single door is out of the question, so the double doors it is." He had discussed this with Sidney many times over the weeks and so his decision was not a surprise, in fact it was expected, and he did not expect Sidney to reply.

Sidney felt his legs starting to sag, they were buckling under the full weight, he waited stoically as Herbie obtained some wedges for the doors.

The 1:20 scale model was robustly built and in consequence heavy. It had taken three months for Sidney to complete and Herbie's supervision of Sidney was intense but lacked constructive comments. Sidney loved model making and needed little prompting, or instructions come to that, it was his baby.

The journey down to the chamber was not without its difficulties, because Sidney had the bulky heavier end, he needed to go down the stairs backwards, experiencing the full weight of the solidly built section of the model amidst Herbie's panicky and disjointed instructions, Sidney knew it would be a nightmare! By necessity it was step-by-painful-step. Fortunately, Herbie had allowed enough time, so they had a well earnt rest after the two hours of hard physical effort. The model was now in place, and at Herbie's insistence, a white shroud covered it completely.

Sidney was looking forward to the presentation, he was pleased with his model and knew it would cause a stir. But there was another reason. Penelope Pride, the case officer, would be there: he liked her. Perhaps his feelings ran deeper than just *like*; maybe infatuation more *like*.

CHAPTER 4
THE APPLICATION

Planning Application 2020/ CRY CITY COUNCIL /6/253/BATTLECRY/1080AD/BCC.

PROPOSED INSTALLATION OF A MEDIEVAL SIEGE MACHINE IN THE GROUNDS OF BATTLE-CRY CASTLE

Committee meeting -- 14th June 2020

In Attendance.

Wanda Longstaff	Chairperson.
Henry Odd	Councillor
Jack Spear	Councillor.
Gwendoline Grace	Councillor.
Digby Pike	Councillor.
Stan Smart	Councillor.
Hazel Hope	Councillor.
Arnold Best	Councillor.
Norman Keep	Councillor.
Dame Nancy Hard-Castle OBE	Councillor
Rose Archer	Councillor.
Billy Bowman	Councillor.
Daphne Darling	Councillor.

Nick Tweed	Head of Planning C, C, C.
Penelope Pride	Planning Department Case officer. C, C, C.
Matthias Oldham	Conservation Officer. C, C, C.

Jasper Thorndyke   Historic England.

Herbert Strange   Architect, Agent and presentation team leader.

Sidney Picket   Design Technician, presentation team member.

Herbert Strange had been commissioned to design a medieval Siege Machine in the grounds of Battle-Cry Castle and linking with Cry church-formally-cathedral. His experience in conservation was renowned, and if anyone could come up with a sympathetic design solution it would be Strange and his right-hand man Sidney. The committee were looking forward to the entertainment ahead; and Herbie never disappointed them in that respect.

The council chamber was galleried on three sides. The ceiling was vaulted and twelve metres high at its apex. For a modern building, it seemed strange to walk into a space so traditional in concept; not dissimilar to an eighteenth-century music hall. The tables for the committee were arranged in an auditorium fashion, each forming part of an elliptical curve. There was a stage behind them for presentation occasions.

The committee members had arrived and were sitting, whispering to each other and nervously, rustling papers. They were pensive and alert; their normal relaxed routine of crunching and dunking biscuits in a tepid cup of tea was abandoned. This was an important meeting and a high level of decorum was necessary, and high court judges never dunked biscuits in public.

Herbie's model stood on two tables put together; strategically placed in the centre. It was covered entirely by a huge white shroud, which was breath-taking in its whiteness as it soared up into the air like a snow-covered mountain. Everyone without exception was in awe and intrigued by this mysterious object. The tension in the chamber was rising, as was the temperature. Herbie's application had created quite a stir, in fact, more of an outrage. The proposal for a twelve-metre-high Siege Machine, now dubbed The War Machine, with a throwing arm reaching up over twenty-four metres into the air, in the grounds of Battle-Cry Castle, was not receiving a favourable response. The public were complaining of the potential danger to the environment; a Hollywood movie set was not appropriate for the city and the noise it would generate detrimental to health. Their objections were like clutching at straws to make a haystack.

The basic concept of having a movable war machine erected in the city centre, sent shock waves throughout the conservation fraternity, and cries of anguish from the Cry Historic Society. And the general public were besieged with petitions and pamphlets which had been distributed far and wide in order to stop this abomination. This aggressive attack focussed public attention, and wild accusations of historic decimation abounded.

The paparazzi were packed into the corridors and staircases leading to the chamber and some clustered in noisy groups in the reception area. Camera flashes from time to time, highlighting and adding brightness to the drama of the white covered secret. The model stood, immobile, waiting silently, shrouded in mystery.

The chamber was full and some of the public were standing around the walls. The atmosphere was electric, as though it were a murder trial. The only sound was the muted rustle of sweet wrappers and an occasional rebellious mobile phone, followed by the accompanying hasty scrabbling and grunts, as the culprit switched it off.

Sidney could see his two Peruvian clients sitting impassively at the back with the general public. The pressure was on; Herbie was now to prove he was worth the high fees he was charging. Sidney knew Herbie excelled under this kind of pressure. He wasn't keen himself and prayed under his breath. He caught Wendy's eye, she smiled faintly in recognition, that cheered him up, he wanted and needed encouragement

Herbie was unflappable, he knew he had a design for a mast, that when presented should give him the standing ovation he so richly deserved, and it must be said, earnestly desired. There was also another reason for his unflappability. It was his personality, he was devoid of any embarrassment and self-consciousness, apart from pride in the manner of his dress and condition of his hair. When dealing with planning committees Herbie took on the stance of a prosecuting barrister; most certainly he would be on the offensive and indeed, would probably cause some deep offence in the process. It would be a battle royal.

Nick Tweed, Cry City's Head of Planning was a man of urbane calmness, a quality most appropriate for his post, and one he used to full effect. He was experienced in dealing with highly sensitive and contentious applications and gregarious committee members. But he did admit to the wife before leaving that morning, that this one took the biscuit. He had locked antlers with Herbie on many occasions and knew what to expect, so forewarned, forearmed, not that it would help him much.

Herbie's application was left to last; the other applications were pushed through at an alarming and embarrassing speed and Wanda-Chair did not hit the table with her gavel once. It was as though the committee were like an orchestra in a theatre warming up for the show. And show it will be, with Herbie the leading actor. That suited Sidney, it gave him time to see that things were going to plan and react accordingly.

Then, at last, the moment they had all been waiting for; Head of Planning, Nick Tweed stood up to address the committee and put Herbie's proposal before them. He spoke with an air of neutrality and with a calm, measured tone that belied his inward conviction. Giving no hint of his personal views on the proposal.

He glanced down, as he spoke, at the four box files of documents prepared by Herbie the agent and marvelled at the sheer volume. His entire department reckoned it was the most wonderful masterpiece of, cut, copy and paste they had ever seen.

Nick looked around as he spoke; "Chair, members, the next application on the agenda is for the placing a medieval siege machine in the grounds of Battle-Cry Castle and Cry church, formally the cathedral grounds and straddling the two roads between." He paused, just momentarily, for the public to digest what he had said.

It was the moment Herbie had been waiting for. As quick as a flash he leaped forward. And with a superb theatrical gesture, one he had practiced at home, he let go the strings holding the huge white shroud draping the towering model. It was a master stroke of stage management and timed for maximum visual effect—it was perfect.

There were gasps of amazement from the public gallery and necks were craning forward to get a better look and this unusual spectacle. The shroud, like a soft gossamer veil, drifted gently down to the floor, as morning mist would drop from a mountain top. The model was now bathed in light; Sidney had rigged up spotlights and switched them on when the shroud floated down. The stage manager of any music hall theatre would have been proud.

Herbie had Sidney make a model of Battle-Cry Castle, Cry Church-formally-Cathedral and numerous buildings in the vicinity including the High Street. Considering the limited time, the detail was amazing. Sidney had set up two tripods with spotlights and the shadows cast upon the model by the lighting angles was dramatic. The Church Siege Machine and Castle Keep, each giving its own distinctive visual impact.

There was an explosion of light as cameras clicked and mobile phones flashed. The media and public alike were in confusion, trying to understand what they were looking at; it was not what they were expecting.

Nick Tweed was taken aback and stopped speaking at Herbie's dramatic actions; he waited for the flurry to die down. Sidney knew this was what Herbie wanted. You need to catch them off guard, the element of surprise, in Herbie's opinion, was a crucial factor in planning warfare.

Nick continued, "Chair, members, in my report I have outlined the reasons why the planning department have recommended this application for refusal. These are extensive and detailed in the report. However, the agent, Mr Herbert Strange, wishes to present his proposals to you in model form. This is not usual, but in view of the controversy surrounding these proposals he felt it important to give a practical demonstration of why the scheme should be approved. Taking into consideration the visual impact and benefits to local commerce." He looked at Herbie and nodded.

Herbie stood up. He had managed to comb the front part of his hair after their sweaty endeavours. But the back was sticking up, like the tail feathers of a strutting cockerel. He walked over and stood in front of his beloved model and faced the committee. In one hand he had a white stick and the other a pencil pointing laser torch. His bowtie was now straightened, and he had a distinct military look about him; a sure sign that there was a battle ahead.

"Ladies and gentlemen," his voice had the condescending tone of a boarding school head boy. "This proposed design for a siege machine placed next to Cry City Castle, will be a unique symbolic statement that will impact the British Isles and be of great benefit to Cry City and the wider community." His voice got louder. "In many ways, and for many years to come." Mouths dropped open at the power of this audacious and nationalistic statement. The throwing arm of the siege machine reaching up shakily to the top of the vaulted ceiling, like the skeletal neck of a Tyrannosaurus Rex, reinforcing their incredulity at the scene before them. The air conditioning unit hummed loudly in the silence that followed

There was then a hushed whispering coming from the gallery that started to grow louder. Wanda Longstaff-Chair spoke out. "Members of the public, please, I would ask for silence?" She nodded to Herbie, who was not at all perturbed by this ruffling of feathers, in fact it was what he wanted, he needed their full attention.

Herbie pointed his white stick at the upper part of the arm. "Ladies and gentlemen, this section of the throwing arm here, is exactly thirty-four metres from the ground to the top when extended. The siege machine runs on a replica of a medieval siege ramp for storming a castle; in the olden days, it would have been called a siege engine." He looked around, all eyes were darting between him and the ramp. "Now, as you can see, it has eight wooden wheels, these are two metres in diameter and one metre thick, constructed of English oak, Historic England were insistent on this, the Normans would have used locally grown oak."

He turned and pointed his white stick at Sidney, and then in an arc, back again to the ramp. Military style, it was his stint in the army, he had seen his commanding officer do it. Sidney, waiting for his cue, jumped to his feet and moved purposefully towards the model. His blond hair, Viking-like, shimmered in the spotlights. His slight, but muscular build taking on a warrior-like stance. The silence was palpable.

He stood alongside the siege engine and reaching out started to push it along the timbered bridged causeway. It was heavy Sidney had decided against using balsa wood, too fragile, he used pine instead. Following on from the first part of the ramp and then onto a timber framed bridge across the road and then finally a ramp up to the castle outer wall. This linked the church-come-cathedral grounds to the castle moat, and ending up against the castle keep outer wall ready for battle.

Sidney pushed the siege ramp along the track until it rested against the castle keep wall, he looked at Herbie for instructions. Herbie nodded dismissively at him, so he stood back.

"Now you see," said Herbie to the many heads craning over the balcony. "We will create a re-enactment of an ancient siege, a seven-hundred-year-old event. It will become a wonderful tourist attraction. User friendly, in that people will be able to access all parts of this ancient structure, giving them a living experience of siege conditions in thirteenth century warfare. Also, it will be a fantastic teaching tool for children and attract commercial activities; a job creation project and major Hollywood style filming location."

His words, combined with the visual impact of the model were having a powerful effect, the silence was profound, the spectators waited for him to continue.

"As you can see, it is movable and has no physical connection with the ground, other than the wheels of course." He laughed to show he had a sense of humour, there were accompanying nervous titters. "There are no supporting stays, or steel wire rigging. It is a fully mobile unit, not a permanent structure as such and more importantly can be easily dismantled, as can the bridge track." Sidney grimaced inwardly at that; he knew it would take a long time.

Herbie pointed his stick high up in the air. "The upper section here is erected on top of the siege ramp below here." He pointed again at the ramp. "This gives an overall height of thirty-four metres, as I have said. This top section I have designed as a slingshot arm, which would have been used for hurtling rocks and stones through the air onto the castle. In the olden days, other unpleasant missiles were also used, dead bodies not excluded." He moved his stick in a dramatic arc to emulate the movement of the sling. He then nodded to Sidney, who standing at the ready pounced forward and operated the sling arm apparatus. Some members of the public were now standing to see the effect, thinking that maybe Herbie was going to throw stones.

He continued, "This is also made of oak and will sit on the upper platform of the ramp and will be at its topmost twenty-two metres above the ground. The height of the bridge track over the mote, is designed so that the attackers can jump over the castle keep parapets. All the health and safety electronics will be hidden, and the required antennae will be in the form of longbow arrows, these will protrude out at various angles, as though fired from the defenders of the castle, you see here." He pointed at the arm at the top: Sidney stood back and they both resumed their seats. Herbie intended to proceed later; he had a lot more to say. Sidney was still puzzled by the nature of the health and safety issues and questioned the reason for it in the form presented; yet another of his suspicions. He could see nobody was interested in health and safety issues—as usual.

Nick Tweed had never experienced a presentation like this before and was taken aback. He stood up and the best he could muster was. "Thank you, Mr Strange, Chair, members, are there any questions you would like to ask Mr Strange at this juncture?"

There was a momentary silence, or one might say a pregnant silence, then the unexpected happened. It was an act of childish cleverness; someone afterwards said they thought it was a newspaper reporter, it was a paper plane made from one of the meeting agenda sheets. It was launched into the air from the public gallery. It was dart shaped for speed, but it was gracefully made and did not dart, but more floated down, as though in slow motion towards the model. There was a titter as it gently and respectfully landed near the High Street on the war memorial gardens next to the church. "Missed," a voice whispered loudly from the gallery.

Sidney thought this funny but dare not show it. He hastily retrieved it with as much dignity as he could muster, before

Herbie exploded and before the titters turned to sniggers.

Wanda Longstaff rapped her gavel on the table. She was speechless at the audacity of it. Herbie, never one to miss an opportunity, shouted, "The Eagle has landed!" He looked around like a circus performer. "And in the right place." This was greeted with a roar of laughter, and people started to clap. This pleased Herbie immensely, but Wanda Longstaff was so enraged she stood up, gavel raised, as though she was going to throw it. She glared at the public then sat down with a face like flint, until there was a long submissive silence, before proceeding.

Wanda Longstaff pointed to Councillor Henry Odd, who was waggling his arm about in the most alarming semaphore manner. Odd was a keen conservationist and a staunch member of the Cry City Historic Society. "I have a question for Strange," said Odd, "Can he inform us how health and safety measures work in this scenario?" He was trying to ramp up opposition. "It looks a precariously steep slope to me for storming up."

Wanda looked at Strange and pointed to Henry. "That's Odd and it would be helpful it you could explain in more detail Strange, to Odd, please." Her old-fashioned use of surnames eliminated any familiarity creeping in—her theory; it also stemmed from her position as headmistress at the local primary school.

Herbie was in his element, his tartan waistcoat was now puffed out, and his yellow bow tie perfectly horizontal. With his white stick, he tapped gently the palm of his left hand. This was a technique he used for getting added attention and to give emphasis to his words. It was the cultivated stance of an accomplished lecturer. It was at moments like this that Sidney admired Herbie the most: like everyone present, he waited.

Herbie's voice was raised, but controlled, excitement and passion flowing as he spoke. "Imagine if you will, the hustle and bustle of our annual literary festival. And then to turn off from the High Street and into the grounds of Battle-Cry Castle and there you will be faced with an amazing sight. The spectacle of a fully blown medieval siege in action." He paused for breath and pointed his stick with his right hand, the other hand half raised in a fencing poise. He quickly continued to avoid interruption.

"There will be hundreds of people, heaving and pulling countless ropes, shouting and chanting to the beat of drums: *real* battle cries. To see the hauling of this massive medieval siege machine up the ramp to the walls of the keep; it will be a fantastic sight. The neighing of horses, sweating and straining under their load. The handlers shouting words of encouragement, and the accompanying crack of whips and of trumpets; bellowing and echoing the chants of war, sending shocks waves of excitement through the city. A real siege with real people." He paused red in the face, but just for a second, then, "Many colourful striped medieval tents for an equally colourful army. The smell of cooking and smoke from campfires. Men and women massing and moving together as an army dressed for battle; it will be a re-enactment to match any epic movie. With the sound of steel against steel and shouts of victory, it will be a sight of monumental proportions."

He stopped, panting with the excitement at this picture he had just painted with words. And then finally; in a hushed reverential tone, "I believe this unique approach will generate enough income to fund a new roof for the castle, and I might be bold as to say: restore the castle to its former glory." He stopped, he was finished, he had put his final nail in the ramp. Then on an impulse said, "I rest my case." He sat down. There was approving murmuring in the public gallery and a tinkling of muted clapping. They were impressed, but reticent to show it.

The committee members were agitated now, and arms were being swung around like windmills to gain the attention of Chair. Wanda Longstaff banged her gavel on the table.

"Members—members—please; consider the facts, we are here to consider a very important application, many businesses and lives will be impacted." Her voice had risen to a crescendo and the members shuffled their papers in order to compose themselves in the silence that followed. Chair then took the initiative. "Please raise your hands all those who are for the application." All hands were raised, including hers. "Please raise hands all who are against." The silence was palpable as the public waited—nothing—just more silence.

"The application is approved." Wanda's voice had a ring of triumph to it as the gavel hit the table. To go against the planning officers' recommendations was a coup.

CHAPTER 5
GOOD NEWS.

The Cry City Chronicle eagerly spread the good news of the council's decision and showed photos of Sidney's model. The public were of mixed opinions, those that were negative, resigned themselves to the outcome of another Cry City mess and said so, others were enthusiastic, especially the traders in the medieval High Street who ventured to suggest a night siege with fireworks. 'It would increase footfall' they said, knowing it would also increase turnover. The day before the newspaper came out there had been consternation among the city shopkeepers. The High Street had been invaded by a Peruvian band and dancers, followed by a group of colourful characters in Peruvian national dress. Apart from the noise, which was loud in a melodious and haunting fashion. They had also brought along a herd of yaks, which left a trail of thick aromatic droppings for the council to deal with and the public to walk in.

Sidney, looking out of the café window, cringed behind his coffee cup. This performance was not what was agreed and certainly not on the day expected. Herbie had arranged the public relations exercise and as usual had left it to others to interpret his inevitably vague instructions. He understood that the singing would be confined to the church grounds, not the whole of the city High Street. The troupe were determined to make an impression and were successful in that respect.

Because of the unusual nature of the project and the fact that Herbie had no other projects, Sidney was assigned the job of project manager and employed by the oak framing specialist, a company called Waney Edge Construction, whose job was the fabrication of the siege machine. The crew had worked on Canterbury Cathedral and the Tower of London and their enthusiasm for all things medieval was infectious. This suited Sidney who was a hands-on type and knew the structure intimately. From the outset, Pinko the Peruvian engineer, who was in effect the client and assigned the project, seemed to lack focus, allowing Sidney to have a free hand. It was his casual approach to the project that confused Sidney, he was there most of the time, he was the resident engineer, yet he was mainly preoccupied with programmes—or so it seemed.

Sidney was pleased for Herbie but concerned about the motives of the client, it was Pinko the engineer who had put doubts in his mind. He decided to push the project forward and get stuck into the production working drawings of the war machine for construction purposes. It would be the first thing that Pinko the engineer would need anyway for him to produce the calculations. What Pinko produced for the carpenters was all a bit rough and ready, he added more timber, but in odd places, which was puzzling, Sidney never bothered to question him about it. Other than that, the man seemed to know what he was doing, in an agricultural sort of way.

CHAPTER 6
POLITICS

Penelope had a text message from head of planning, he wanted to see her about the War Machine Project. She felt nervous, Nick Tweed's text was a little too formal for her liking, but he smiled as he asked her into his office. He had a conference table and they sat opposite each other; he had a file in front of him. "You know Sidney Picket quite well I believe?" He smiled again, but this time softer.

Penelope felt uneasy. "Yes, we meet up often." She felt her face reddening, she waited.

"Good—good. I want you to put a proposal to him Penelope." He looked at her intently and grinned. "Don't worry I'm not asking you to propose marriage." She giggled nervously and felt confused. She knew he was doing his best to make her feel comfortable.

"No, it's about the siege machine; I am getting mixed messages from the applicant, the Peruvians. They came to see me yesterday and expressed concern about Sidney Picket. It was an awkward meeting and they asked me to keep a close eye on him. They are aware he is now working for the contractor, but they don't want him interfering with the duties of their on-site structural engineer a man called Pinko, there's no record of a surname, just Pinko." He looked uncomfortable and to avoid eye contact opened the file. "I was wondering if you could have a word with Sidney, purely off the record you understand, this project means a lot to the City of Cry." He smiled disarmingly. "Its politics, you know how it is." She didn't but thought it wise not to say so.

She left Nick's office with mixed emotions; firstly, she couldn't imagine Sidney interfering and secondly, she felt it unfair that Nick was using her to bring him into line. She felt the Peruvians were being manipulative and sneaky with it, was it because Sidney posed a threat in some way. She could see now why Sidney was suspicious of them, the council should be impartial, and Nick was being used by the councillors. She decided to play the Peruvians at their own game, but she must see Sidney first.

She met him in the war machine site office after work, she felt nervous, but ventured a small kiss on his cheek. He reddened and smiled, she launched into her story to hide any embarrassment. "I have just come from a strange meeting with Nick Tweed. I thought I would wait to see you rather than phone." She relayed the facts, Sidney looked puzzled, she thought he would be angry.

"That interesting," was all he said, he sipped his coffee before continuing. "The only person who is interfering is Pinko, their engineer, but I get on well with him, their claim is spurious, I have only helped to speed things up, Pinko is not that efficient." She could see he was analysing the situation; he spoke slowly. "I wonder what they are up to?"

"Can I make a suggestion?" Penelope was keen to put across her idea. "I think you should play along with the engineer, go out of your way to be helpful, he will know you have been told to do that by Nick. You can then ask him innocent questions, he won't see that as prying, more team building on your part." She grinned mischievously. "Nick told me that he likes you, no surprise there." She grinned.

Sidney leaned back in his chair. "Well, I must say you have thought this through Penelope, and I agree, it's a good plan—actually I like Pinko as well, so it makes things easier." She was relieved he had not taken her suggestions as interference. She found him open and amenable to new ideas and suggestions, she was getting to know him better and liked what she found.

"Let's take a walk." Sidney said. "It's getting claustrophobic here, so many things to think about." She knew it must be challenging being in the thick of it. They found themselves walking along the embankment towards the bridge. "I am getting more confused by the day." His voice strained. "The Peruvians are taking control and reluctant to let the rest of the team know what they are doing or thinking. It's all a bit bizarre." She was glad it was a nice warm sunny day, there was an element of freedom in strolling along, but they mustn't be complacent, the situation was too serious for that.

"May I make a suggestion?" Penelope still felt uneasy after the mysterious meeting with Nick. "We can meet officially, I would suggest at my office, you can then ask me formally for advice and I can respond and record what we have spoken about, that way we would have a record to challenge the Peruvians with, if necessary. Keep it professional—what do you think?"

"Good idea." He sounded relieved that a plan was coming to fruition. "We can send copies to relevant parties and tease out a response, we will only be seen as us doing our job and we can't get criticised for that, and maybe it will reveal more that we think."

They both stood still and looked back at the castle, its impressive battlements towering over the river. "Well, you know my feelings Sidney, I think Herbie's been naïve, and obtained a planning permission that the client can manipulate to advantage, but what is the advantage, that is the question. Certainly, I cannot object to the change taken place, I have no grounds." They continued walking and Penelope slipped her arm under his, he squeezed it, she was happy, their friendship was blossoming.

CHAPTER 7
THE PERUVIANS

Herbie would like everyone to think the siege machine was his brainchild, as he thought so himself. medieval war history was his speciality and the client's idea had quickly become his own. Sidney had realised by the copy emails from the Peruvian Chief Executive of Goth Enactments in London, that they were leaving the project in Herbie's hands. Their input, as the client, was confined to requirements concerning the size of the siege machine, details of the slinging arm and its alignment to the castle wall. Sidney felt that they were being forceful in this respect and happy to leave the working solution to Herbie and their engineer. Even so, this show of trust seemed suspicious to Sidney, who could think of other more pressing issues for them to be concerned about, but maybe it was their reliance on Pinko that gave them this confidence.

Sidney kept a low profile in the early stage, waiting for Herbie's interest to wane, and as usual this didn't take long, his attention span was limited. Sidney could then take over and run it the way he wanted, after all he was now effectively working for the timber framing company. Herbie had an arrangement with them and would be relieved of the burden of paying Sidney for the duration of the contract. Sidney hoped that his doubts would fade away as he immersed himself in the project. Jamie, one of the head carpenters, said they would appreciate his pre-planning advice; Sidney had designed the structural sections to be transported when dismantled. Herbie had cleverly shoved, along with Sidney, the total responsibility onto the framing contractor.

The Peruvian client proved to be generous in their financial contribution and did not question the budget put forward by Herbie. Their only suggestion was the involvement of local colleges to encourage teaching, it all sounded good to Sidney, too good, the nagging suspicions refused to go away.

CHAPTER 8
THE CHIEF EXEC

Sidney had always given Herbie due respect, at least as far as his conscience would allow, but sadly, if he were pressed to admit, there were more bad traits in Herbie than good. It was a harsh conclusion to come to, but Herbie's propensity to arrogance and vain glory, was in Sidney's eyes certainly not good, and most certainly bad. To a limited extent, Herbie's superior demeanour gave him an advantage, but this façade soon faded in the face of genuine, superior knowledge. Sidney learnt quickly that in order to keep his job and sanity he never argued with or challenged Herbie. All the professionals that knew him agreed that Herbie was unteachable. He confirmed this by taking his normal self- opinionated view, that, if it wasn't his idea it must be a bad one. Sidney was annoyed that Herbie couldn't attend the coming meeting, after all he was the clients' architect, he suspected boredom and he was going on holiday.

The progress meeting with the Peruvian client present had been arranged for that morning at nine a.m. on site, it was the first time the client had attended. They were now three months into the contract and on target, even though there were many extras. So, Sidney was expecting an amicable gathering and had invited Penelope along, this wouldn't be unusual, after all she was a council authority representative. Sidney was more than happy with progress, but to his utter dismay, things did not go as expected. It was the Chief Executive of Goth

Enactments Limited, a Mr Alfonso Jose. The atmosphere changed the moment the man entered the site office. His black eyes glittered like precious stones out of the fleshy folds in his brown mottled skin. He was not an attractive man. He was barrel chested and though he was short his shoulders were broad, and his powerful presence dominated the room. His mouth was set in a cruel permanent shape and showed no emotion other than to convey a sense of superior disdain.

Pinko, the engineer, looked uncomfortable; his normal affable demeanour had changed to a furtive subservience. It was obvious he was intimidated by the Chief Exec, who had sat himself in a chair at the end of the table directly facing Sidney. The three carpenters working for Waney Edge Construction, sat on Sidney's right, with Penelope and Pinko on his left. It was Sidney's job to run the meeting.

Sidney was relieved that Herbie was on holiday, but now, having met Mr Jose he had changed his mind; Herbie's skin would have been thicker under the baleful, brooding gaze of Mr Jose the Peruvian enigma. Sidney gave his account of the previous months' progress, including the discovery of woodworm in some of the oak, too much sapwood was the carpenter's complaint. Pinko knew about it and the oak was condemned and sent back. Sidney confirmed this had caused no delay. He thought he would get this in before Pinko scored points. The carpenters supported his statement with consolatory grunts of acknowledgement.

"The only problem we have now," continued Sidney, his voice raised, "is the axle grease for the eight main wooden wheels on the machine, the axle is solid stainless steel and one hundred and fifty millimetres in diameter. As we know each wheel is two metres in diameter and one metre thick to take the enormous weight. To counteract this and stop the axle bending, Pinko has designed a solution to this problem, by placing identical wheels directly above and fixed into the main structure. He placed Pinko's drawing on the table. "As you can see these will be covered by leather skins to hide them, it is a modern innovation, but the weight is the deciding factor: this is now signed off by the engineer and by the council." He didn't bother to remind them that medieval war machines were built as light as possible in order to move fast, hundreds of people pulling ropes were vulnerable to attack. We probably need a thousand to pull it now he thought but decided to keep quiet about that.

Sidney glanced at Penelope, who faintly smiled encouragement. Jose the Chief Exec stared impassively at him for a moment then said. "How much do these wheels cost?" His voice was guttural and condemning. There was an awkward silence, they all looked at Sidney, who, having had extensive experience in dealing with Herbie, responded in his best urbane manner and delivered his response with panache.

"The problem we have, Sir," he emphasised the title and swiftly continued, "as Pinko will confirm, is the extra weight of the internal accommodation, floors and equipment." He paused and looked at Pinko, who was sitting upright and looking down intently at his note pad—no help there then, thought Sidney.

"The cost is an extra £3,000.00 per wheel, so, eight wheels, that's £24,000.00 plus VAT" Sidney stared back at the Chief Exec and waited for a response, thinking this was a cheap price to pay for creating the opportunity to build nearly nine thousand square feet of moving office space. The man's impassive face crinkled dramatically and his glittering eyes all but disappeared. The Chief Exec had smiled, then his whole body began to shake. It took some moments for Sidney and the others to realise that the man was laughing or trying to. Everyone looked at him and then at each other, except Pinko, who was staring at his boss in dismay. The stocky man's shaking subsided and he became passive again, he then spoke.

"VAT," he growled. "Mr Herbert Strange informed us there was NO VAT to be paid." His thickly accented voice emphasised the, NO. Sidney's heart sank, this was typical of Herbie, telling the client what they wanted to hear rather than the truth. The Waney Edge Company operatives were looking puzzled, their company was charging VAT and paying it. They looked at Sidney, he was in charge.

Before Sidney could make comment, Pinko decided to say something. "We can email Mr Strange and ask him if Her Majesty's Revenue and Customs have cleared this." Sidney was relieved, he worked for the Waney Edge Company now and VAT was payable. The Chief Exec seemed satisfied with Pinko's suggestion but said nothing, appearing to be waiting on proceedings.

Sidney decided to continue. The meeting went smoothly after that, dealing mainly with technical matters, he hoped Penelope wasn't bored. Then, near the end of the meeting, the Peruvian Chief Exec decided to attract everyone's attention. He loudly tapped the top of his pen on the table repeatedly. "Lady and gentlemen." He said loudly; there was a stunned silence. "I have a statement to make." He then turned quickly to Pinko and spoke rapidly in Peruvian, Pinko rigorously nodded in response, he then continued in English.

"My company, Goth Enactments, will be joining forces with a film making company to cover the coming events, and the works you are doing; they will not be intrusive and will be most helpful to you. That is why we need the extra internal space in the siege machine; we need to cater for some of their filming equipment and other facilities."

His little speech was succinctly delivered for maximum effect and obviously rehearsed. It was a plausible story, but Sidney didn't believe him. The equipment for professional filming was normally contained in mobile units and articulated lorries with supporting accommodation and designed to travel. To house this activity in the siege machine was not practical for filming, he thought it prudent not to voice any opinion, but make practical suggestions instead. We can conceal all the power cables under the ramp," he said, with a touch of false enthusiasm, and as the siege machine will move very slowly with manpower, we can use some sort of drum, I am sure Pinko and I can come up with a solution." Pinko nodded enthusiastically.

The Chief Exec grunted. "Good, you agree then." He turned to Pinko. "Inform Herbert Strange of this new arrangement will you."

Pinko nodded. "Yes Mr Jose." The meeting was closed, and Sidney thanked them for coming. The two Peruvians left in silence and did not shake hands, the carpenters were a jovial bunch and left chatting away about their next task.

Penelope and Sidney sat alone, he grinned at her. "What did you make of all that Penelope." He sat back and looked up at the ceiling for a moment, then sighed. "I must remind myself that I am working for a contractor now and just doing my job. The way I see the situation is Herbie has abandoned me and sidestepped his responsibility and seems to have lost interest in the project, so why should I worry?"

Penelope smiled grimly at him. "It's because we both know that something is dreadfully wrong."

CHAPTER 9
THE TREE

Penelope, drawn to the aroma of toast and coffee, dressed and descended to the kitchen, her mother insisted on sending her to work on a full stomach, which she was grateful for. "What are you up to today Penny?" Her mother's standard morning statement, from which she didn't necessary expect an answer. Penelope was looking forward to the coming site meeting, she had never met the Chief Exec of Goth Enactments. "I have a meeting at the Castle site today, a big cheese is coming— should be interesting. She dared not mention Sidney, romantic assignation's, particularly hers, would set her mother off, it would be her favourite topic every morning for weeks.

She arrived at the meeting early, and she thought the workforce a jolly bunch. Sidney was the perfect host and supplied drinks and biscuits. They sat waiting for the arrival of the Peruvians, they arrived on time. They entered the site cabin silently, with no acknowledgements and sat down. Penelope liked Pinko he was an amenable sort, but the Chief Exec, well he was in another league altogether, she thought he looked positively evil and gross with it. A man you would not want to upset.

The meeting went along reasonably well she felt, but was surprised at a film company being involved, but of course publicity was always good for the locals and their businesses. She was however left with an uneasy feeling, her training as a planner alerted her to the signs of manipulation taking place. She was relieved when the meeting closed and she hadn't been challenged in any way; she felt sorry for Sidney, he had split loyalties, but she thought little of Herbie leaving Sidney to cope, and felt he didn't warrant loyalty from anybody.

The meeting finished at about ten fifteen and Sidney suggested they go for a stroll, to mull things over he said, they found a seat in the castle grounds. "Frank said to report back on any developments." Sidney sounded worried. "I guess this filming business is a new development. I think this whole business is getting complicated and very strange, that Jose gives me the creeps." He paused. "I feel we are getting involved in something fishy Penelope, and no mistake.

"Why don't we go to the top of the castle, it's a nice day and I do have a council pass, it's an official visit." They made their way up, both had visited before, but never together. They stood at the top gazing at the panorama. The city spread before them and the River Cry snaked its way down to the sea. Cry City church, with its lead covered spire rose, towering amidst the myriad of ancient multi coloured tiled roofs. Sidney said he thought it easier to see the bigger picture from this vantage point, maybe give them a better understanding of the Peruvians' plans and aspirations.

They peered over the ruinous castellated parapet and looked down at the route the siege machine would take as it besieged the castle. "Do you see that ancient tree over there." He pointed to a large sprawling lime, its drooping, aged bows supported by varied and numerous timber poles and acrows, set upright at strategic positions. "We mustn't cut that down; the tree officer would be most upset; the siege ramp will have to circumnavigate it."

Penelope knew the Cry City Councils tree officer, Micky Birch, she had crossed his wooded path before, and found his bark was just as bad as his bite. Every living tree and shrub within his domain he regarded as family members and his children and must be fiercely protected at any cost. Tree protection orders, TPOs, were issued by him at the drop of a hat. The story goes, that he once issued a TPO on a timber telegraph pole that was covered in ivy. Birch is always getting his wires crossed so what's new, a councillor was heard to say at a council meeting.

She relayed the story to Sidney, he laughed. "I know Herbie doesn't like him, but I don't think we have any trees to worry about and the grass will grow back." His next comment was a challenging one for her. "You know the inner workings of Cry City Council Penelope, how much sway do the Peruvians have, Nick Tweed made it clear they have his ear, he's a good politician." She hesitated answering, Sidney was right in many ways, it was complicated and all a bit of a mystery.

CHAPTER 8
FRANK.

Sidney had finished his Saturday morning stint at the construction site amidst the piles of oak and the fragrant aroma of sawdust and shavings. The war machine was taking shape and the public were appreciative of access to view progress. Penelope was waiting for him in the small church garden adjoining. It was a warm bright day and Sidney found her sitting on a bench under the canopy of a huge yew tree, a beautiful girl and a beautiful day, thought Sidney. "Hello," he said. "Hope I haven't kept you waiting." He paused and smiled. "I mentioned—I agreed to meet someone here for ten minutes I hope you don't mind; he should be here shortly he wants to give me some leaflets on green oak. I tried to put him off, but he was persistent." He sat next to her.

"That's OK." Her voice was soft, quiet. "We have the rest of the day." They sat facing the huge sheeted scaffolded structure that hid the war machine. "It's going to be impressive Sidney, that's for sure."

He was about to reply when a voice came from his right. "Mr Picket—Mr Sidney Picket?" He turned to look up at a tall man, casually dressed, which seemed to enhance rather than detract from his powerful physical presence. His face was bland, not a flicker of emotion. "Thank you for seeing me at such short notice." They both stood up.

"Frank Miles." He offered his hand. "And you are

Penelope Pride I presume."

She smiled. "Yes, hello." She blushed. He then shook Sidney's hand. Sidney wondered how he knew her. He waited for a lecture on oak, none came, what happened next was a surprise. "I would like us to go somewhere quiet, I need to talk with both of you, it's important." His voice had a disturbing ring of authority to it. Sidney looked at Penelope, they could use the site hut, but for her protection a public place would be better; this man worried him, he had a look of a man of action.

"There is a coffee shop near here," said Sidney, "Five-minute walk away." The man nodded in agreement. They walked in silence towards Don's place. It was an awkward silent walk; the pavement was only wide enough for two abreast.

Frank was gracious and allowed Penelope and Sidney to walk ahead, "You know the way I'll follow."

The coffee house wasn't busy, and they were able to find a convenient table for them to talk privately. Sidney felt nervous, his casual ten-minute meeting with an oak rep was turning into something different. He decided to let Frank take the lead: Don supplied the coffee efficiently. "Penelope, Sidney," Frank's voice was slightly raised, "I have a confession to make, I am not who I said I was." He paused and looked intently at them. "My name is correct, but my knowledge of oak is limited to a walk in the woods." A flicker of a smile crossed his face, but quickly faded.

"I work for a government department; national security is my speciality." He produced his wallet and opened it to show a government stamped card with his face and name on it. He let it linger under their noses to demonstrate his intentions were honourable.

Sidney was hot with excitement; the man was SAS and with the War Department. "Is this about the war machine?" he blurted out.

"Quite right Sidney, may I call you Sidney?"

Sidney nodded. "Of course." He looked at Penelope. "I think we need to hear what Frank has to say." His voice was neutral. "He might have some answers for us."

"Oh." Frank looked surprised. "Answers, to what sort of questions?" Sidney felt uncomfortable.

"Firstly, I think Penelope and I would like to understand a little more of your mission, if that is the right term."

He was a strong character Sidney thought and used to giving orders rather than taking them, however he responded graciously enough. "I can only tell you a little, but I will say this; the company you work for have plans for the war machine as you call it and it not for the reasons you think." He paused, waiting for a reaction.

"Oh." It was Penelope's turn. "How strange, we have been wondering why things were so odd lately."

"I am not surprised," he said, "I am a total stranger to you and so I would expect you both to be wary, I apologise for meeting you in this fashion, but it was imperative that my position was kept secret and so I needed to cut across protocol." He then produced two cards from his wallet and gave them one each. Sidney was impressed with man's credentials: Captain Frank Miles, OBE Special Armed Services HMG.

"Thank you," said Sidney. "This must be serious then." Penelope was silent, Sidney sensed that she was at a loss for words. Frank Miles responded.

"Well yes in a manner of speaking; my team have been

keeping the site under surveillance for two weeks now, sorry about that but it was necessary. I will explain; the problem we have is Goth Enactments, it's a new company formed we believe for the project, but the two directors and chairman are known to us. I will say just this about them, they are not known for their charitable deeds and we are sure they are up to something, but not sure what." He smiled again. "Normally the local police would deal with this sort of thing, but this is different. These men are in a league of their own; they are clever and resourceful and big players in the criminal fraternity. It was the planning permission that alerted us, it was a mistake on their part using their real names at Companies House, Pinko is still a mystery to us."

Penelope spoke up. "May I ask? Why are you speaking to us?"

He leaned forward more relaxed now. "Yes of course, firstly Sidney is close to Mr Pinko and they have a working relationship, this means that information can be gleaned from this. You Penelope know all the various people and disciplines involved being the Planning Department, Conservation Officer, Historic England, Highways Department and a few more I am sure. So, you will be able to ask questions without arousing suspicions. Can I rely on you both?"

They agreed, but Sidney, though going along with it thought it bizarre to the extreme, but it was exciting so he would see.

CHAPTER 9
VAT

Having finished his email report that he would send to Frank, Sidney copied in the minutes of the site meeting with the Chief Exec he forwarded a copy to Penelope; he decided to wait for her response before sending it on to Frank. It was obvious that their suspicions were well founded, but the fundamental issue remained unanswered, why had the two Peruvians deliberately created an atmosphere of mistrust? The answer to that eluded them for the moment.

It was obvious that the Peruvians were clever, or maybe fiendishly clever, would be right description. Penelope agreed that the report covered everything, and he sent it off. He got a response from Frank within the hour so he telephoned Penelope. "Frank wants to visit us on site tomorrow, he said he would pose as a VAT inspector, but he did sound as though he was joking." He chuckled. "looks like things are getting hot Penelope, I feel sure he will enlighten us more tomorrow."

Frank arrived at nine fifteen next morning, they were waiting for him. He appeared jovial enough, for their benefit perhaps. "Thank you for your report Sidney, most helpful." He avoided small talk and got down to business. "I mentioned before that Mr Alfonso Jose is known to us, my department have a file on him, he is also under investigation for other misdemeanours." He opened his shoulder bag and produced a folder and opened it. "This is a photograph of him attending a demonstration in Parliament Square." He pushed it across the table. "He is overtly anti British and doesn't care who knows it; he is sailing very close to the wind."

Penelope looked at the photo taken of him at the demonstration. "He looks even uglier, photogenically speaking, and Sidney will confirm the man's appalling bad manners." Frank looked at her, then Sidney, he smiled. "I take it you don't like him then. I can say you would be joining a long queue. Our net is closing in on him, but he does have friends in high places." He sat with a file open in front of him. "VAT returns." He smiled knowingly. "I need to explain something to you both; Mr Jose is unorthodox in his dealings and a dangerous man. We were surprised when we found out that he had surfaced and attended your site meeting, he normally keeps a low-profile business wise, particularly on the legal front."

They sat saying nothing for a few moments, the noisy squawks and cries of the sea gulls settling on the scaffolded tin roof far above, enhanced the silence that had fallen on the meeting. Frank continued, there was now an urgency to his voice. "The reason I am here today is to alert you to the danger and seriousness of the situation. We do not know what Mr Jose's intentions are, but I can assure you it will not be for the good, for yourselves or anybody, he is an evil man, with evil intentions." He placed some more papers on the table. "It is quite clear to our department, that from the amount of money being spent by Mr Jose's company, that this is not a viable commercial venture, the figures don't stack up—the returns are not there."

Frank placed a spreadsheet on the table in front of them. "These figures are based on the information given to the planning department in support of the planning application. It's the confidential forecast for the anticipated revenue generated by the visiting public to the war machine, visiting families experiencing the atmosphere of real medieval fighting from the inside of the machine, a real enactment with the sounds and smell of battle. This is now gone and, in its place, sweet smelling offices! Totally ridiculous." He collected his paper up. "I suggest you both keep your heads down, concentrate on doing a good job and stay alert. The fact is, there is nothing we can pin on Jose now; keep me posted; I would suggest we meet in a weeks' time, unless something urgent turns up. In the meanwhile, I will be doing some more digging."

Sidney then realised that Penelope and himself had been too close to the situation to see clearly, but Franks overview had confirmed the validity of their suspicions. They agreed it would be a good idea for Frank to see the site from the top of the castle before he left. Sidney's head was buzzing with questions as they made their way towards the castle keep. There must be another agenda, another reason for building a medieval War Machine, but what was it? As they walked, a thought floated down gently into his mind, like a petal of enlightenment. The War Machine he was building, was this a real war machine? It was a bizarre thought, but how could it be used to wage war? This was 2020, the age of technology.

Sidney would keep his irrational thoughts to himself for the moment, time would tell; the whole thing could be some sort of scam, the Chief Exec looked the sort.

CHAPTER 10
SIEGE

Penelope had a reasonable workload but decided to find time to research all available files on the war machine application. There might be something more relevant to the current situation, maybe something that was not so at the time. It was mid-June and a bright sunny morning, she had spent the last two hours going through Herbie's consultants' documents and feeling a walk would be nice, when she came across a small document relating to the alignment of the war machine and ramp to the castle keep itself. Pinko the engineer had been quite specific about the angle of approach that the machine should take, it was 242 degrees south west. These figures seemed to jump out at her, but why was the precise angle so important. She felt sure a medieval army wouldn't be that scientific about sieging a castle.

She copied and scanned the document for Sidney and Frank, maybe they could shed some light on it. The next document was the method statement drawn up by Pinko and attached to this were ancient ordinance survey maps. Sidney must have seen these she felt sure, but she emailed them both copies, it might help. She then picked up the most recent document from Sidney and his attached drawings of the siege machine. She lay one of the drawings out on her table, it was he side elevation of the war machine. It was then that she realised why people alternated between calling it a siege machine and a war machine, Sidney's drawings were all annotated war machine, but the application was described as siege machine.

She sat back, sipped her coffee and studied Sidney's drawing, prompted initially by the fact that he had drawn it. Then she felt the hovering slinging arm had taken on a shape she hadn't noticed before, it reminded her of something—but what? Then an image came, of course, the Triffids in H G Wells' *The War of the Worlds*, long necks and a body not dissimilar to what Sidney had drawn. The idea grew stronger in her mind, from the top of the neck, being the end of the sling and the bucket that threw the rocks, the triffids would send their powerful beam to destroy all in its path. A War Machine to end all War Machines.

Penelope felt excited, her imagination was working overtime, she must speak to Sidney about this, but would he laugh at her? Then the issue discussed with Sidney, why did Goth Enactments want the slinging arm hollow? She couldn't help wondering and thinking on the sinister side of things. She decided to get a copy of The War of the Worlds and read up on Triffids, also a DVD on one of the original films—it was an idea that would not go away. She was determined to think it through before sharing with Sidney or Frank; if there was something in her theory, better not let it be pushed aside.

CHAPTER 11
WAITING

Sidney had plenty to do, so welcomed Frank's suggestion, head down work hard and play innocent. The next four weeks had been hectic, six more carpenters had been employed to create the four levels inside the pyramid shaped structural frame. These four levels would be for the office space, and progress was good. Means of escape was sorted out, on the basis that—a building on fire trundling along a track, would be a logistical nightmare for firefighters. The solution was—a sprinkler system throughout the whole structure, even the toilets. In the name of authenticity, the fire officer agreed to let them have the hose reel fitted on the back of a horse and cart, which would follow the siege machine along. But he also wanted a standby emergency holding tank with a pump mounted high in the structure. A tall order thought Sidney, who didn't have much time to contemplate on the darker side of things, he had decided to wait and see what Frank would turn up with.

Pinko was proving to be a friend, of sorts, and clearly wanted to be liked. Sidney found him helpful and amenable to suggestions, they had a pleasant working relationship, which helped to ease the pressure. Pinko had been wrestling for two weeks now with the problem of the ever-increasing weight of the siege machine, Sidney had lost the will to live on that one. Pinko eventually come up with a solution for the weight increase on the eight massive oak wheels, which put Sidney's mind at rest.

He had redesigned the wheels and inserted a two-metre diameter cast iron wheel, sandwiched within each of the eight heavy oak wheels. These would run on railway tracks set into the ramp. Sidney liked this idea; it stopped the machine from wandering off the ramp. This was great news, but expensive, nobody seem the least bit bothered about cost and Pinko signed it off as usual and the money came through promptly. Sidney was wondering if he would be getting a bonus when the job was completed; Herbie never paid bonuses.

Frank was very keen to see any technical information produced by Pinko on mechanical and electrical services, it was important he said. He sent through what he had by email, there were so many ducts, wires, and computer cables, he couldn't make any sense of it all. It was the beginning of the fifth week after the initial meeting with Frank and six months into the contract. The total expenditure to date on labour and materials was just over 1.7 million—and increasing all the time.

Frank suggested another meeting on site, but this time he would like to bring a colleague, they agreed for this coming Monday. The machine structure was now complete and ready for the external cladding. To be authentic, it would need to be protected from the fiery arrows of the defending foe. They all agreed; rows upon rows of colourful fighting shields would be fixed to the external face of the sloping walls; it would certainly look the part.

Sidney often wondered when the Chief Exec would turn up again, Pinko didn't know and avoided talking about him, perhaps he might be a little more transparent later, he would need to be patient. It was now late-June and the weather, was gloriously hot, all the men were grateful for the scaffolded covering. Frank arrived promptly on the Monday morning with Alan Berry, a scientist working in Frank's department. Frank would still be the VAT man. Penelope was able to come, which was a relief, Sidney still found Frank a little intimidating and two government agents might be too much of a handful.

Alan Berry turned out to be the complete opposite to Frank. He was dapper in appearance and middle aged, and to add spice to what would normally be a sombre occasion, he had a keen sense of humour. His opening remarks set the tone. "Greetings from the City of Londinium, my lady." He bowed to Penelope, who graciously curtsied. "And my Lord."

He offered the top of his hand to Sidney, who did not kiss it and was a little taken aback, but managed a "Hello, Lancelot, where's your shield?"

Frank roared at that, not to be beaten Alan carried on. "Anyway, nice place you've got here, I would do a stretch on the rack for this."

Frank was grinning broadly and sensibly took the lead. "It's good to see you both again, I can see you have made great strides, it really is looking great. Thanks for emailing me the progress images, they were most helpful." They made themselves comfortable around the table.

"I do like the smell of fresh oak," remarked Alan. "Reminds me of camping in the woods." Frank put a folder on the table, a hopeful sign, thought Sidney, that he had information for them.

"Alan would like to ask you both some questions first, then have an inspection of the machine." He looked at Alan

Berry, who had become a picture of sobriety.

"Yes, well now, from the images I have seen and the service drawings you sent to Frank, there is one major question I have, or should I say statement. I do not understand the logic in producing many complex wiring looms for simple office accommodation. The computer system is there and is a simple standalone wiring system, with lighting and power the same, the rest of it is seriously complex and expensive." He paused, the three of them waited for him to continue. "I would be interested to know the professional background of the electricians who did this. The wiring installation has the same feel and characteristics as a nuclear submarine, and I have worked on a couple of those." He looked at Frank. "You're right Frank, this is serious stuff, shall we go and have a look?" He went to get up.

"Could we leave it for a few minutes," said Sidney. "Their tea break is at ten, and that will give us half an hour, hopefully that will give us enough time. We must assume the electricians are in on it and we don't want to raise suspicions. Just so you know Alan, Frank is our VAT inspector and you are now promoted to Health and Safety Officer—and that's no joke."

It went according to plan, much to Sidney's relief; Alan took lots of photos and talked continuously about health and safety issues and disasters he had experienced. Shortly before they had embarked on their tour, he had pointed to something, then put the same finger to one ear, then his mouth and mouthed, 'bugs' silently—they got the message. Sidney was shocked, why didn't he think of that? He wasn't trained to think that way, but he was learning fast. Professional criminals are mysterious creatures, devoid of conscience, empathy and compassion, he would need to be extra vigilant from now on.

CHAPTER 13
THE ELECTRICIANS

To counteract the forces imposed by the thrust of the sling arm, which could throw a ton, Pinko had carefully designed the massive oak framing. By putting emphasis on and increasing the sizes of the timbers at the rear of the war machine, he found the calculations worked for stability. "We need to test it Sidney, this is like reinventing the wheel." They were having a design meeting and they both knew of course that the arm would only be throwing balloons, but the same problem emerged, how to be authentic, but be practical.

"I wonder what the building inspector will say," said Sidney. "He thinks we are a wacky bunch as it is."

It was agreed that the external wall of the war machine structure should be clad in thick seasoned oak planks and the carpenters were well underway with the work. They said it would take another three to four weeks to complete, the planks being so thick.

When the war machine structure was complete, Sidney had planned to have all eight carpenters working on the ramp. It would be one hundred and twenty metres long and fifteen metres wide. A section had already been constructed for the war machine to be built upon. He was beginning to relax, things were going to plan, putting devious politics aside. His complacency however was short lived, there was a serious argument between the electricians.

The electrical contractor was subcontracted to Sidney's firm but worked directly for and paid by the client. There were three electricians, it was the youngest one that was the cause of it. He was a burly, surly young man of about twenty-five years of age. Sidney would probably have let them get on with it, but the carpenters had complained. Pinko's view was clear, Sidney's role in the project was contracts manager—so manage!

The next chain of events would be challenging for Sidney and not a little disturbing. He made his way to the area where the electricians were working; the carpenters were hovering in the background, clearly Pinko had told them that he would be dealing with the matter. He approached the burly electrician; Sidney, as usual was neatly and cleanly dressed, his high-vis and a new helmet. He was over six feet tall and whilst slim, was well built. The electrician was about the same height, but broad in the waist, and scruffy. He wore no health and safety gear and stood, staring sullenly at Sidney as he approached.

A rebel without a cause if ever there was one, thought Sidney. "May I have a word?" he asked politely, he stopped about a couple of metres from the man.

"What do you want?" The tone of the man's voice matched his surly demeanour. Sidney decided not to pussy foot around. "You are not wearing a helmet and high-vis jacket, this is against health and safety regulations, is there a reason for this?" There was a silence, all the men were waiting for the electrician to react, they were not disappointed.

The man took two steps towards Sidney, his manner was threatening, his face was red with anger and his arms raised gorilla fashion. "What are you going to do about it?"

Sidney punched him with force in his expansive stomach

using his right fist. The man gasped, then groaned and staggered back, Sidney looked calmly at the two other electricians and said quietly. "I want this man off the site immediately, he is a danger to himself and the workforce, if he refuses, call me." He turned and slowly walked away. He resisted looking back, he could hear scuffling going on and more groaning.

The reaction to the violence hit him as he walked back to his office, he felt weak at the knees, it was the adrenalin rush. He was shaking a little but managed to make himself a cup of coffee. He regretted his action, but knew it was inevitable, his tolerance level, when dealing with bullies was nearly zero! It was something he struggled with, but could deal with it most of the time, Herbie was an example. But when it became physical, well that was another matter.

He was left alone for a couple of hours, then a knock on the door. "Come in!" his voice raised.

It was the two electricians; they entered looking uncomfortable. The older one spoke. "We are more than sorry for what happened Sidney, the man's an idiot." He looked at his colleague. "You did something we couldn't do, so thank you for that, he's gone now and for good. Our boss knew he was a bully and we can assure you he will not be back; we have seen to that." Sidney was relieved, the consequences of his action could have been dire, but he judged that the three were doing something illegal and would want to avoid a brush with the authorities—of any sort.

Sidney got up and shook their hands, he had gained their respect, and that could be helpful in the future. He decided to carefully nurture the beginnings of a relationship, they were bound to be wary of him from now on and he hadn't forgotten the bugs.

CHAPTER 14
THE COMMITTEE

A request had been made to the planning committee chairperson, Wanda Longstaff, for the committee members to pay a visit to the trebuchet to view progress. It was Dame Nancy Hard-Castle OBE, her ancestors, on her mother's side, were French and she thought trebuchet was a much more dignified and genteel description for the war machine; Norman Keep, not one for mincing his words thought she was a snob. It was about time there was a visit, Norman said, his constituents were nagging him for an up-date.

It was left that Penelope would organise it. Normally she disliked the task, it was stressful and the members fickle, but with Sidney there it would be nearly enjoyable, he was yummy and had an important quality for occasions such as this—a sense of humour. Sidney had told her Herbie would attend, which should add to the level of entertainment. It was agreed that the visit would take place on a Saturday morning at ten. The day arrived, it was overcast and drizzling, Penelope was relieved the project was under the huge scaffolded sheeting. Sidney was well dressed as usual and made his high vis look like it was from a Saville Row collection; Pinko was nowhere to be found. Herbie was subdued and appeared wandering aimlessly about, head down.

They all arrived, reasonably on time and congregated on the ramp in front of the war machine. As they talked between themselves, their voices slowly became reverent whispers. The war machine towered above them, massive and intimidating, as though demanding respect. This was the first time that Penelope had seen the committee members impressed, there was none of the usual scathing remarks. Apart from Daphne Darling remarking. "It's awfully big!"

The war machine was festooned with many different shaped fighting shields. Sidney had organised a local art academy to paint them all, he told Penelope there were over a thousand. Historic England were happy with the various designs, these depicted the heraldic images of power through the ages, as long as it was colourful, they didn't mind stretching the truth a little, after all it wasn't as though there was a real war going on!

"Gosh," exclaimed Billy Bowman, gazing up at the hundreds of overlapping shields. "It's certainly colourful, looks like a giant armadillo."

Henry Odd stepped closer. "Great isn't it, what do you think Darling?" Daphne Darling giggled. "What an Odd thing to say, but it is impressive I must say." The others gathered closer, waiting; Sidney took the initiative, Herbie still wasn't his normal self and showed no interest in the proceedings, Penelope was pleased, Herbie would only cause confusion by his sarcasm.

"Now, if I can have your attention please." Sidney's voice was strong and calm. "The important point to notice in the placing of the shields, is the overlapping method used. This is designed to deflect the arrows fired down from the battlements towering above, and the shields are closer together and denser at the front of the war machine. The main fear was burning arrows, these could cause devastating fire damage."

Penelope could see the members were mesmerised by Sidney's passion, he continued. "Those defending the castle would probably have concentrated their firing on the hordes of attackers pulling and following the war machine as it moved slowly towards the castle walls, and pouring boiling oil and hurling stones upon the sea of moving shields protecting the mass of bodies struggling beneath. Now we can only imagine the noise and the smell of it all, but our intention is to recreate this in every authentic detail; an exciting challenge to create a marvellous experience for the visiting public." She knew Sidney had taken a leaf out of Herbie's book, it was the fiery delivery. She wondered if Herbie was pleased with his performance, she noticed he still looked dejected.

Sidney waited for a response, it came from Arnold Best, the romantic. "It must have been a herculean task." He piped up. "Pushing, shoving and heaving this heavy contraption along the ramp slippery with blood and gore, and the screaming must have been horrendous."

Nancy Hard-Castle OBE, endeavoured to counter Best's convincing, emotional outburst by shouting. "The sounds of singing and chanting war songs of encouragement more like." It was uttered with a competitive passion.

Penelope could see the magnificent war machine had stirred the nationalistic fervour of the committee, and Sidney lost no time in adding more fuel. "You can imagine," he shouted. "The noise of the horses and drums, insistently beating for victory."

It was Jack Spear who responded spontaneously. "And the womenfolk shouting and screaming encouragement, just like the suffragettes"

It was at this moment of rising passions that at long last

Herbie Strange gave utterance; his voice was raised in a weak, but clear battle cry—though no one knew which side he was on. "The victory is ours."

There was some muted clapping and murmurings of, "Hear, hear."

Penelope could see that Sidney was relieved and he proceeded to usher them all into the war machine. It took time for the group to wander and climb through the labyrinth of interconnecting rooms and Billy Bowman and Rose Archer got mysteriously lost, that was their excuse. It was at moments like this that Penelope could see how the British nation, with committees such as this, had colonised the world.

It took a while to gather them all together again, Bowman and Archer were irritatingly elusive; weekend shopping was next on their agenda.

CHAPTER 15
BOB

Frank telephoned Sidney; it was a short call but one that would radically change the course of events; Frank wanted to assign one of his SAS men to join Sidney on site. "He will act as night-watchman. I suggest you use the excuse of having expensive equipment around and the structure is now a serious fire risk and twenty-four-hour security presence is needed, our man will operate through a local security company, I will finalise the arrangements if you are happy with it all. His name is Bob Bloom, I think you and he will get on."

Sidney felt comfortable with Frank being in control, the whole situation was bizarre. He was locked into an odd set of circumstances, in control of the construction, but not of the finished article; the sling arm was to be delivered soon and he certainly wasn't in control of that, the company that made it would be fitting it. The whole process was getting more challenging by the day. He quickly got Pinko's approval for the cost of security and the scene was set.

Sidney warmed to Bob immediately; he had popped in to check over the site and meet the task force. He had a likable personality and a bright smile—however—he looked like a tough security man who would take no nonsense. His uniform fitted like a glove and his slim waist emphasised his broad shoulders. Sidney took him away from the office cabin, he was convinced it was bugged, he decided to take him to Don's coffee house. "I start tomorrow night," said Bob. "If your office is bugged, I will find it, it will be my first task, Frank said this job was right up my street, I have a background in electrical engineering, I have the testing equipment, so I shall be kept busy, Frank has given me an idea of what I am supposed to be looking for.

Sidney was pleased that as everyone slept, the wheels of security rumbled on. He met up with Penelope after work and brought her up to date on Bob their new security man, but he was concerned about Herbie. Penelope agreed that something was amiss. "When you were talking to the committee on Saturday," she said, "I noticed that Herbie was constantly looking at his phone, I know that can be a habit for some people, but the way he was looking at it seemed strange to me. He spoke into it several times, I couldn't hear but the tone of it sounded heated, he looked really worried."

Sidney sighed. "I've known him for quite a while now and this is the first time, I have seen him rattled, perhaps he has had a health scare, it does happen. Since I have been working for the contractor, we have lost touch with each other, maybe that's it." He looked out of the window vacantly. "Why does life have to be so complicated?" He took a sip of coffee. "Shall I ring him now and ask him?" She nodded and smiled, he found his number and rang it.

He answered immediately. "Hello Herbert, how are you?" Sidney said and waited, nodding and smiling at Penelope.

Herbie's voice was subdued. "Fine, Sidney, thank you, how are you?"

"Well, I am fine, but really I am ringing about you, to see how you are. We have lost touch with each other over the past couple of months, I have been busy, but I notice you seemed a little preoccupied and perhaps worried when you attended the meeting on Saturday, I'm just concerned, that's all."

There was a silence then Herbie spoke. "I think we need to meet up Sidney, as soon as possible, I have some serious news for you."

Sidney was taken aback. "Oh, OK, when?" His response was sharp.

"Let's say tomorrow at mid-day at Don's coffee house."

"Fine see you then." Sidney terminated the call and sat in silence for a moment.

"He wants to see me tomorrow and said it was serious." They finished their coffee in silence. "I'm looking forward to Bob starting," said Sidney, as he walked her to her car. "You will meet him soon, I like him, I think he's the perfect person to be watching our backs."

CHAPTER 16
JASPER THORNDYKE

Historic England had taken a proactive and forceful role at the planning stage, but because it was a movable structure, any possible objections would need to be readdressed when the war machine was up and running, hopefully along the track. Jasper Thorndyke, the assigned Historical England officer, was an aloof sort and tried to avoid the nitty gritty of an argument, he preferred a distant sparring, a warfare of emails, of which, it must be said, he was a master.

The storm that was brewing came to Penelope's notice through an email from Nick Tweed, his diplomatic request could not be ignored, she was asked to find out what the problem was. She was at first mildly surprised, this soon turned to concern. Jasper had taken umbrage. It was Pinko, his response to Jasper's well-crafted political emails, was brutal and dismissive. She rang Sidney, he told her that he was learning some Peruvian swear words from Pinko. "What's happening Sidney? Jasper is livid, says Pinko has insulted him, he refused to say more, but will be taking the matter further. Nick told me to investigate, but it's difficult with Jasper sulking. I believe it's all about some not so funny emails, have you seen any?"

"No," replied Sidney. "But Pinko is here, I will talk to him and get back to you, this needs to be sorted out, we need Jasper on our side." Sidney had heard Pinko shouting earlier through the glazed screen that separated their offices. All was quiet now, he walked over to his door and knocked, Pinko beckoned him in. "Hi Pinko, is everything OK?" The man's face was a picture of suppressed anger.

"No, everything is not OK. That Jasper Thorndyke character is not in the real world. This is a commercial project, not a real war, with real deaths and real blood. But let me tell you there will be real blood if this carries on." He was breathless from discharging his stress.

"What did Jasper say in his email?" asked Sidney, hoping, forlornly, that there may have been a misunderstanding.

Pinko glared at his computer. "Here, look, this is what it says—I will read it to you—'Dear Mr Pinko, he says, I am writing to you to express my deep concern at your company's complete lack of respect as your non-compliance demonstrates. It was agreed, as stated in my statement supporting the project, that you would not, I repeat, not throw missiles of any shape or form at the castle walls. This wilful act of vandalism will damage the historic stone fabric and cause a loss of our heritage. Dame Nancy Hard-Castle OBE informed me that it was stated at a meeting on site that you intend to throw stones and other deleterious matter at the castle walls. This is unacceptable—I repeat unacceptable.'

Pinko paused for breath, his face still red, then continued with end of Jasper's dirge. 'I will be obtaining a signed affidavit from Dame Nancy Hard-Castle OBE and when this is available, I will obtain a high court injunction to stop the works…' Yours Sincerely… etc. Pinko sat back and closed his eyes, a mournful look on his face.

"Oh dear," said Sidney, not quite sure of what to say, he would need to choose his words carefully. "I think Dame

Nancy Hard-Castle has been quoting me. I gave a talk at the site on Saturday and she was there, I described the very thing she is claiming she thinks we are going to do, but I am afraid she was only half listening, I was describing the methods used centuries ago in medieval warfare, the helium balloons we are going to use is not medieval. It's a mistake on her part, I was quite clear in my talk." Sidney hoped that this would calm things down a bit. The last thing he wanted now was trouble with Historic England, and he did think Jasper was too quick off the mark and his rapid response ill-conceived and badly timed. "I agree with your email Pinko, the man needs bringing down to earth, he should have consulted the team. I will follow it up if you like, it's a lamentable lack of respect." This seemed to placate Pinko, who was clearly relieved at this turn of events. This project is getting more bizarre by the day thought Sidney, Penelope was also relieved, and this would get Nick Tweed off her case.

CHAPTER 17
ARM LESS

Pinko had been reticent to give a delivery date for the sling arm, he said it was design problems, Sidney had the suspicion that he didn't want him to see how it was being made. It was six months on and not a murmur from Hoist Electronics, the company fabricating it. He would have preferred a visit to their workshop, but Pinko was in charge and he had lots to do anyway. A couple of days later, Pinko declared that the sling arm was now complete and would be delivered later in the week. "Sorry for the wait Sidney, but you know how these things are." Sidney didn't, but left it at that, it was coming, that was the main thing.

Sidney did notice how pensive Pinko was, maybe he was nervous, it had been a long time with the manufacturers and there were many changes along the way, mainly it would seem by Pinko. To make and design a hollow stainless-steel lattice design slinging arm for a medieval war machine, some twenty-four metres long and finished to look like English oak, was no mean undertaking.

The next challenge was to arrange an inspection by Jasper Thorndyke of Historic England. He could be the most demanding of critics, he would want to score points now, particularly after Sidney had caught him out and humiliated him with the Dame Nancy Hard-Castle debacle. Penelope said he could be vindictive when in a sulk, so be prepared for a challenging time.

The twenty-four-metre-long slinging arm was fabricated in two sections, principally for ease of transport and general handling. A crane was organised and ready on site. Bolting the two sections together and erecting the sling into position would be a delicate operation due to the covering of the stainless-steel skeletal frame. This was finished in painted fabric for lightness, like the covering used on First World War aeroplanes. He was impressed by the colour and wood printing on the fabric. The two sections looked the part, like two massive pieces of oak. "When they are bolted together and in position high in the air." Pinko said. "I defy anyone to say, it isn't oak." He was clearly pleased with the result. Sidney complimented him on the design and said it was a success.

The next stage would be the assembling and fitting of the arm into position. Pinko fussed about the positioning of the crane, he had hired it for a week, so there would be no rush and hopefully no mistakes. The height to the underside of the scaffolded tin roof was twenty-five metres, plenty of room to practice the art of slinging rocks and hidden from the inquisitive and prying eyes of the general public.

Sidney studied the arm and was mystified by the complexity of it. The mechanics and electronic systems were bewildering and completely beyond his understanding.

Not so for Bob. "This is a sophisticated bit of gear," he said, he had inspected the arm sections that night and was sharing an early cup of coffee with Sidney. "I am not surprised you are confused Sidney, this is state of the art technology, space age stuff, NASA would be proud of it." He looked out of the office window at the war machine, it was an hour before the workforce arrived. "Sidney, I cannot imagine what they want to use this for, but I can assure you, slinging helium filled balloons is an excuse. There is something more sinister going on, Frank said he has an idea, but would rather I do my homework first before putting forward his hypothesis.

Sidney had to agree with him, that spending of some two point seven million pounds on a massive wooden truckle was hardly a commercial proposition. "None of it makes sense at the moment." Bob mused. "But time will tell, I have a lot more digging to do."

CHAPTER 18
THE STRANGE AFFAIR

There was a lot happening on site and a complication from Herbie Strange at this juncture would not be helpful, after all he was the architect of the situation and his concept. Sidney sat waiting; it was precisely twelve noon when Herbie appeared. Sidney was shocked; even to look at him was stressful. His manner of dress, though expensive, was ill fitted and oddly disjointed; his hair was dishevelled and his face anxious, blotchy and flushed.

"Hello my boy," he said breathlessly. A flicker of a smile crossed his face. "Thank you for agreeing to meeting me at such short notice." He sat down solidly with a marked lack of grace. Sidney felt uncomfortable, Herbie had never thanked him for anything all the time he had worked for him, this must be serious.

"That's OK Herbert, how can I help?" Sidney's calm, composed demeanour seemed to ease the tension, but Herbie still looked around as though he wanted to escape. He brushed the clean tablecloth with his hand and adjusted the cutlery, slowly, fastidiously.

He spoke quietly. "Hopefully you will not think too ill of me my boy." He leaned forward slightly to give emphasis to his damning statement. Sidney was feeling decidedly and increasingly nervous. Herbie continued with gritty determination. "My confession is made even more difficult for me due to my lamentable lack of repentance. You see, I do not think I have done anything, what you might call terribly wrong, yet my conscience tells me I have, and I must also confess to be in torment about it." He paused and Sidney felt a little relieved, it might not be that bad, but Herbie had a furtive look as though he were being followed.

"What on earth have you done Herbert, or think you have done?" He looked at him, his face was a shade of grey and putty- like.

"I lied." His words were short and sharp. "I lied because I desperately wanted the siege machine project, I needed the money."

Sidney didn't want to hear this, the man was baring his soul and clearly in torment, but why pick me for confession, thought Sidney and what had he lied about? He decided to be positive. "How can I help?" wanting to sound like a friend; Herbie was self-centred among his many other oddities, but he was honest and to admit to lying must have cost him dearly. He was beginning to feel sorry for him, a notion that was strange to contemplate, considering the man's past arrogance.

Herbie leaned forward over the table like a Guy Fawkes conspirator, his voice lowered, even though the coffee house was nearly empty. "Firstly Sidney, I want you to promise me that what I am about to tell you, you will not breathe a word of it to anyone."

Sidney nodded, "Of course not," he replied, hoping he wasn't getting into deep water.

"Two years ago, I was commissioned by the owner of a medieval house located near the castle to prepare a full measured survey, it's called Castle Ditch House, you might know it. The building was empty, and therefore easy to use a laser. I scanned most of it, but the basement was so full of junk, so I had to measure that by hand." He then smiled, rather sadly Sidney thought. His voice then took on a stronger tone. "I then made the discovery of a lifetime, I wanted to tell you at the time Sidney, but couldn't risk the secret getting out." He paused, the furtive look returned; Sidney wondered what on earth the secret could be. "If you have time Sidney, I would like you to do something, rather than explain; have you time?" Sidney was surprised at the eagerness in his face.

"Yes of course," replied Sidney. "Sounds intriguing."

The building was down an alley off the High Street. It faced onto the castle and its moat and the area of land linking the church. Herbie took a bunch of keys and a large torch from his shoulder bag. He followed him into the building, which had been neglected, there was dust and old papers littered about.

"This way," said Herbie. They made their way down to the basement. The musky aroma of damp plaster and old brickwork was pungent, there was no ventilation, no air movement.

"Over here." Herbie shone his torch at the end wall of the basement. "I put the furniture back to hide what I had found, it's the entrance to a tunnel." He put the torch on a shelf and started to pull away old chairs and other debris. Sidney helped as best he could, and they cleared it away. Herbie then took the torch. "There it is." Sidney could see a large gap in a damaged and rotten partition. It had been constructed of lath, plaster, and flimsy timbers, "It crumbled when I touched it," said Herbie. "Someone sealed up this entrance many years ago, I moved a chair against it and it just disintegrated."

He shone the torch into the gap, Sidney was shocked and excited, it was an entrance to a tunnel.

"This is amazing, Herbert, what an exciting find, who owns the building." He didn't reply. The smell of the darkness cloyed about them and the flickering beam casting strange shadows, making his response even more mysterious.

"When I show you what the tunnel leads to, you will understand why I lied." He slipped sideways through the gap in the partition, Sidney followed close behind. The arched tunnel was constructed of stone and looked like early Norman; the floor was covered in large flagstones.

They moved cautiously forward and after just a few paces the floor started to slope rapidly downwards, and the ceiling followed suit. Because there were no steps it was difficult to determine the depth before the floor levelled out again. They continued silently, Sidney could think of nothing to say, it was a weird experience. It was the height of summer outside, but chilly and wintery down here, Sidney shivered. "Not far now," said Herbie. The tunnel was coming to an end; there was just a black hole ahead and hushed stillness. Sidney's heart began to race, this was awesome, what had Herbie found?

Sidney felt he was missing out and wanted to concentrate on the detail; he wished he had a torch. They stepped out of the end of the tunnel into pitch black darkness. Their eyes slowly adjusted to the limited power of the torch; it was a huge cavernous space. Herbie's flickering darting torch revealing a huge vaulted under croft, they could not see the end of it with the torch. And wide, again difficult to tell, maybe fifty metres there were many columns with lofty stone arches forming the ceiling.

Herbie's torch flickered aimlessly into the ancient space; he spoke. "You see Sidney, when I saw this, I was entranced, mesmerised, so I bought Ditch House; I now have sole access to this marvellous space." There was pride in his voice as he moved around shining his torch. "There is one problem however, this wonderful underground vaulted structure is directly underneath the ramp that carries the war machine. As you know there have been changes and I was becoming increasingly alarmed when Pinko insisted on increasing the weight of the war machine structure and now it's a moving office block. It will be a national disaster if this goes ahead; the vaults are not capable of taking the weight."

They stood there in the deathly silence; both aware of the implications of Herbie's discovery; no wonder Herbie was stressed thought Sidney and now he was complicit in the scheme of things.

CHAPTER 19
BIG NEWS

Sidney hadn't returned her text message, Penelope wanted to meet for lunch, with Sidney at the coal face she felt out of it. She phoned instead, he seemed distant somehow. "Anything wrong Sidney?" She hoped she didn't sound pushy, but the thought that he might be drifting away nagged at her, her insecurity showing through, she blamed her mother.

"No, of course not." His voice was perky, she sensed he was being upbeat for her sake. "Penelope, there has been an interesting development, unfortunately I have been sworn to secrecy, so for the moment I need to honour that." He paused. "Well just to say it's a bit more than interesting, I would say exciting. You said you would like to meet for lunch, that would be great. In the meanwhile, I will check again to see if the person who told me would be comfortable with me confiding with you, sorry just being courteous—it's quite serious."

Penelope was taken aback, what could this mean and who was the mysterious person he needed to talk to? She would need to be patient. They met in the usual place; Don greeted them with a beaming smile; it was obvious he thought they were an item, which pleased Penelope. They waited as he fussed about preparing the table for them and then taking their order.

When he had gone Sidney became excited? "Herbie was the person I told you about and he agreed I could share it with you, but no one else." He spent the next quarter of an hour giving her the weird story and showing her some of the images he had taken on his phone of the medieval under croft.

"That is incredible," she said, "If Jasper Thorndyke of Historic England found out there was vaulting the size of a large supermarket under the grounds of Battle Cry Castle and the church, he would let the whole of England know."

Sidney laughed. "All in good time; the first consideration we have is; how does this impact the war machine project?" Herbie's view is, the ramp must not be built over the vaulting, and indeed must be some distance from it."

Penelope could see the implications but felt she should visit the vaulted under croft before making judgement. She found Sidney's account so amazing, it was unreal. "I have the keys to Castle Ditch House," he said, "I can show you, but first I want us to walk over the land it's under, it will only take ten minutes, but it will give you a better feel for when we go underground; its located between the castle and the church.

Later, they made their way to the basement; the tunnel entrance was straight ahead. She felt nervous now.

"This is a bit creepy." She shone her torch into the darkness.

"You will be fine," said Sidney. "You wait and see what's inside."

They made their way along the tunnel and walked into the huge underground space. Penelope was in awe, words failed her; the war machine project paled into insignificance compared to this. This was no re-enactment, this was real. They both agreed that this discovery changed everything, it would most certainly put Cry City on the medieval map.

Herbie would have some explaining to do and Nick Tweed would not be impressed, shock waves were about to be unleashed on Cry City Council, in fact the whole of England and the wider world. This is national news: Penelope wondered if she should have her hair done.

CHAPTER 20
MEETING

Sidney thought it prudent to break the news to Pinko first before going public, that way, from a PR point of view, they would be showing solidarity and demonstrate professionalism. Herbie's plan, having unleashed his dramatic find onto the public, was to diplomatically withdraw from the scene, in the forlorn hope that focus would not be brought to bear on the reason for his purchasing Castle Ditch House and more importantly when.

Pinko took the news surprisingly well, in fact he was quite unperturbed. Sidney spread the site plan out on the table in Pinko's office. He had marked up the position of the siege ramp in blue and the approximate position of the medieval vaulted under croft in red. Pinko leaned over the drawing, Sidney was conscious of the man's knowledge, he would be looking at it with the eye of an experienced structural engineer.

"You are saying we can only get this close to the wall of the castle keep." Pinko pointed his finger at a red line, the point where the underground vaulting started.

"Yes, Pinko," Sidney replied. "Historic England will be most sensitive to encroachment, so we think it prudent to be cautious, not necessarily from an engineering perspective though—just politics. I am sure you could design a bridge to it closer. It's the weight of the siege machine, the tonnage is massive now." He felt sure Pinko didn't know what it was or hadn't bothered to calculate it. "If we had a collapse it would be a national disaster." He looked at Pinko waiting for a reaction, he had painted a black picture deliberately.

"Oh," he said, he paused obviously contemplating on the logistical implications, his response was surprising. "Is that the extent of the problem? Well, I am pleased to tell you there is no problem." He smiled smugly. "We can terminate the ramp at a point well back from the edge of the vaulting; now, how far is that away from the castle keep?" He produced a scale and measured the distance. "Yes, as I thought, we can cut the ramp short at that point and still reach the castle walls with our missiles. Yes, we can easily do it; the company who made the slinging arm I feel sure will confirm it, it has been factory tested." He walked back to his chair and sat down, obviously feeling in control. Sidney was seeing another side to the man, but wasn't quite sure what it was.

Sidney was confused, Pinko's reaction was not what he was expecting. Confining the war machine to a short run of track should have been a major set-back, but no, it was business as usual, apart from the mass of media attention and public interest. Pinko was good at reacting on his feet and looked quietly smug at his dealing with the matter. Tomorrow was promising to be a hectic day, the public reaction to the find would be real news.

CHAPTER 21
CONDITIONS

The email came from Bob, it concerned Pinko. He had prepared a formal departmental statement for Frank and sent it on. Sidney studied this on his laptop and could see Bob had done his homework. It was all a bit daunting, but he took comfort in the fact that it was the British government and they had the resourses, and also hoped they would take any blame.

The document was simple, factual and thorough. There were three statements however, that he had underscored each for special note. The first: Mr Pinko gives the impression of a slightly eccentric and dithering engineer, whose attention to detail is woefully inadequate. I feel he has cultivated this persona to hide his true nature. The second: Mr Pinko has falsified the technical information relating to loadings of the electrical power supply that's connected to the national grid and that generated by the on-site power units. Why did he do this? The third, which was the most disturbing of all: Mr Pinko is not who he says he is. Nobody knows what his real name is, he is an engineer and a competent one, but that is all they know of him. The rest of the report was mainly information relating to Goth Enactments Ltd which wasn't much.

Sidney was pleased, Bob had discovered crucial information, he wondered what Frank made of it. He emailed a copy of Bob's report to Penelope. Then before he had time to digest it, let alone discuss it with Penelope, Nick Tweed wanted to see Penelope and himself urgently. His secretary arranged for them to come in later that morning. Penelope was waiting for Sidney in the council offices' entrance foyer. Penelope was obviously concerned, and agitated, Nick was her boss after all. "I wonder what he wants," she said, "It can't be about Bob's email—could it?"

Sidney felt sorry for her, she was a professional and the shenanigans they were involved in were not that. "It must be about the war machine, otherwise we wouldn't be invited together, don't worry you haven't done anything wrong, don't be nervous." She smiled weakly. Nick's secretary took them up to the top of the building and showed them into Nick's office. It had magnificent views of the river; the sun had dissipated the early morning mist and there were some pleasure boats moving about, Sidney wished he were out there.

The first thing that startled Sidney was Nick's other guest, it was Pinko, what on earth was he doing there? He was sitting at the conference table, he rose when they walked in, there was no formal handshakes, a bad sign thought Sidney.

"Thank you all for coming," said Nick. "May I suggest that I table the reasons for why this meeting has been called, I have prepared a brief agenda." He handed the sheets around. "You will see I have covered the four basic concerns that the planning committee have expressed, I shall talk through these if I may." Nobody responded, they waited for him to continue. Sidney and Penelope looked down at the agenda, Sidney wondered if she was thinking the same, this was like a faint echo of the email sent by Bob. His heart started to race, was there a connection?

Nick Tweed started to address number one. "Goth Enactments are concerned about the date for the official signing off for the completion of the works, can the council officers confirm the methodology of information required." Nick looked at Pinko. "Mr Pinko requires this conformation urgently; his company is spending a considerable amount of money." He turned to Penelope; she was ready.

"The practical completion is one thing, but Jasper Thorndyke of Historic England must also formally agree in writing and so do I; does that address Mr Pinko's concerns?

Sidney was impressed with her response. Pinko nodded, but not convincingly. Nick continued, secondly, the members want assurance that no undue ruckus and loud parties will be held in the war machine." Pinko didn't respond but made notes. "Number three, this is an extra condition, but one that must be complied with, all the rubbish generated by the war machine activities must be cleaned up by Goth Enactments Ltd." He smiled at Pinko. "Number four, the council valuer is still trying to work out how to calculate the rateable value of a moving office block, he said he would get back to me, but it's a moving target."

There was a silence at that moment Sidney realised that Nick Tweed was playing games, but not with them, with Pinko.

Nick made it clear the meeting was concluded, he appeared to be anxious for them to leave. Sidney was relieved there was no mention of the vaulted under croft or getting a revision to the planning permission for altering the ramp. He was pleased to escape with Penelope.

"Nick was up to something," said Penelope. "Pinko thinks he has what he wants, I think that was his aim, he didn't want to ruffle Peruvian feathers."

CHAPTER 22
DELEGATION

Penelope decided to try and keep a low profile, she munched her cornflakes and contemplated on the day ahead. She desperately wanted to talk to her mother about the situation, and Sidney said he would like to meet her. But she knew the barrage of questions, that would unleash, would carry on for months. There was a big meeting today, so she put off that challenge for another time.

Nick Tweed convinced Herbie that a select group of people should visit the vaulted under croft. "It will be good for your reputation Herbie, being a conservation specialist and you could conduct the tour yourself."

She visited Nick in his office that morning. "I have agreed the list of people to attend our meeting at Castle Ditch House Penelope, if I could run through this with you." She looked at the list, "Firstly, I feel all the committee members should be invited, also Jasper Thorndyke of Historic England, yourself and Sidney with your two guests, they are security people I believe and that's it, though I think some members may not be able to attend, there should be about eleven altogether, very important to keep things as tight as possible." He grinned, she was pleased that he was agreeable for Frank and Bob attending. "I must say I am looking forward to it Penelope, a very exciting find indeed."

They had collected outside Castle Ditch House; Herbie was standing at the front like a doorman and dressed appropriately. "Thank you all for coming, I would ask that you be prepared for an interesting experience." They followed him into the building and through to the kitchen where the basement door was. He opened it and the excited chattering died down as the group filed one by one down the basement stairs. Penelope was relieved to see Herbie had arranged lighting by using a series of wandering leads.

They all arrived at the bottom and clustered around Herbie. "Now," he said, his posture taking on a dignified stance, "may I suggest we keep fairly close together, but in single file please, as we go through the tunnel. Jasper will be in front, and as a specialist in historic buildings and structures, he will need to take his time and assimilate the facts before him, so your patience please." Putting Jasper on a pedestal was a good tactical move, thought Penelope. She didn't rate his power of observation, but he was good at writing reports for those who were.

They were all too excited to take umbrage at being told what to do by Herbie. Dame Nancy Hard-Castle OBE trailed furtively at the rear; Jasper Thorndyke was still smarting over her misleading information on the throwing of missiles, he felt she was throwing her own mud. Frank and Bob were in the middle of the chain, behind Penelope and Sidney. Whilst the tunnel was wide enough for two or three people to walk side by side, Penelope could see the wisdom in single file, you were able to see more of the structure.

At the end of the tunnel, the group filed quietly out into the massive vaulted space, with its many stone columns fading into the distant darkness. There were gasps of amazement, and exclamations of: "Oh my goodness." And, "This is incredible." And a whispered, "It's like a film set for a Dracula movie."

Herbie had done his best with the lighting, but the space was so immense. Penelope noticed that the group were clustering together; the darkness was intimidating and the chill of the damp, still air made the experience even more eerie. Jasper had lost his exuberant arrogance and hovered in the centre of the group, I expect he's frightened thought Penelope, smugly, he has bitten off more of history than he can chew this time.

Curiosity not quite satisfied, the group meandered slowly, reluctantly towards the tunnel entrance and daylight, then the silent procession was abruptly halted. It was Daphne Darling, she cried out, it was a cry that would change the destiny of Battle-Cry Castle, Cry City and all that dwelled within. "Come look what I have found." Her voice now raised to more of a squeal. They quickly gathered around her as she looked down. "See here." She pointed down at a huge stone slab forming part of the paved floor. "It's the entrance to a vault dated 870, look it says a Saxon king is buried here." They all knew Daphne would be the darling of Cry City from now on.

There was a stunned silence; in the chilled air, the mist of their joint breathing hovered over the gathering. For centuries historians have wondered where he had been buried. Daphne Darling's face was gleaming with excitement. "This is wonderful." Her voice breaking with emotion. "This will change everything; we can get grants." They all knew that as Cry City's treasurer where her heart was.

The group began to discuss the discovery with some excitement, but this was soon dampened down by Jasper Thorndyke's series of jaundiced comments. Penelope knew he was miffed that he hadn't discovered the vault himself, but he was hiding away in the group. Jealousy is sickness to the soul, she had heard that somewhere, or was it hope deferred.

CHAPTER 23
PINCER MOVEMENT

Frank and Bob wanted a meet up as quickly as possible. The visit to the vaults had meant that their tactics needed to change, Penelope preferred an evening meeting, Nick Tweed was being demanding at the office. Sidney picked her up and they drove to the riverside pub. Frank and Bob were sitting outside under a parasol, the evening sun was still warm. It was an ideal location for a peaceful rendezvous, thought Sidney, but the subject matter was less than peaceful.

Frank took the lead. "Thanks for getting us an invite to see the vaults, Penelope, an amazing discovery I must say. This should deflect attention away from our enquires, we need to spend more time researching the real reason for building the war machine. Bob has drawn up a plan, but before he shows us that, can I ask, where is the model of the whole project you presented to the committee? Could be useful in looking at the bigger picture."

"The model is at Herbie's office, but I have a three-dimensional image on my computer," said Sidney. "I can walk you around the site and fly over at any height, shall I download a copy for you, it includes Castle Ditch House, I have my computer in my car with me, so any time." Frank looked pleased.

"That would be great, after the meeting then." Sidney was intrigued,

"What are you thinking?" he asked. Frank turned to Bob's plan. "Perhaps you would like to run your suggestions past us Bob, it may shed some light on things."

Bob produced a red marker pen. "Well, the way we see it is this, it is obvious that Pinko is not concerned about the length of the ramp and the distance of the war machine from the castle, so this leads us to the question of the war machine ramp and importantly the distance from the end of it—that is the new end—and the castle keep." He paused and adjusted the drawing for them to see better. "So, if we can consider the ramp for the moment, having studied the submitted design and access statement for the planning application, it is quite obvious that the intention was to run the war machine up close to the castle walls to effect authentic siege conditions, this concept has now gone, so the planning permission is not being complied with and Goth Enactments don't seem to mind. And from what you are saying, they are happy with the new shortened ramp." He sat back and looked at them intently. "Now for the puzzling part, it concerns the alignment of the war machine ramp. The records show that this was an important design feature and Goth Enactments were firm about this. Now, this alignment is not affected by the shortened ramp, and so I have come to form a theory, and please it is only a theory, but it may kick off some ideas of your own." He leaned forward and was becoming more animated. "From the data I have studied and bearing in mind the criminal minds involved, I have come to the conclusion that they, that is Goth Enactments, are putting in place some sort of weapon." Sidney was stunned into silence, they all were.

Bob turned a page in his notebook. "My theory became more plausible the more I thought about it, and as time went on the facts certainly are doing so." As he was speaking, Penelope remembered her thoughts of ten weeks ago of the old sixty's film War of the Worlds, and how the image of the fighting machine depicted in the film and its similarity to Sidney's war machine had disturbed her, she shared this with them.

"There." Bob's voice raised in excitement. "Another confirmation that we need to think outside the box.

Sidney woke up at that. "I was wondering a few days ago if it could have anything to do with microwaves, I know that pilots are cautioned about flying over satellite communication towers. Apparently, the reason I have read is, if the pilots stay too long over it, they may have their posterior cooked." There was nervous giggling at this, but they all knew they were dealing with a dangerous unknown and fiction can become fact.

Frank and Bob looked at each other, obviously the conversation was going in the right direction, each of them was visualising the head of the sling arm, spitting invisible fire power, but at what, at what cost and why?

There was a silence as they sat in the sun, the warm breeze sending the scent of summer wafting over them. A normal, innocent experience to which they were oblivious, wrapped in the mental turmoil of their disturbing discovery. Nobody wanted to voice it, but Penelope did.

"What shall we do?"

CHAPTER 24
UNVEILING

Pinko seemed to be gathering confidence and in turn was pushing Sidney. He wanted the sling arm fixed in position and working and had little interest in the ramp construction, which, to Sidney was also crucial. Sidney had to try and believe he was working for a political activist, not a mild-mannered engineer. He was also expecting a visit from the mysterious Chief Exec Jose, he seemed to have gone off the radar.

They had one of their disjointed weekly meetings where Pinko, as usual, avoided any detailed discussions relating to the sling arm. Sidney had long ago given up probing and left the investigations to Bob's nightly sojournings.

"I have decided on a public demonstration," said Pinko. "Now the arm is fixed in position and the war machine is fully functional and watertight. So, Sidney, we can now remove all the scaffolding." He seemed pleased at his authoritative statement. Sidney was the employee and could only but agree. Though he felt a bit more time with the war machine under cover would be better, he could see the merit, it would add impetus to moving the project to final completion.

"That would be good, Pinko," he said, "we can also finish off fixing the shields in position; do you think we should contact the press?" Pinko was clearly pleased at Sidney's positive response to his, what could only be interpreted as an instruction.

Sidney knew from Bob's report, that the complex electrical installation was not yet complete, and in the meantime, he was having an in-depth study of the function of satellite masts, there might be a connection. Maybe Pinko and co, were trying to get valuable government security information of some sort, his imagination was working overtime.

It was now six weeks to the official completion date, Pinko had added a further three weeks as a buffer. And apart from the internal engineering, electrical and mechanical the war machine was practically finished. The outstanding item was the ramp, which was now considerably shorter. Sidney was becoming increasingly uneasy; they were now moving towards completion and still no concrete evidence of Goth Enactments real intentions. It was clear now that the prime objective of entertaining the general public, as originally intended, had been abandoned; so, what now? It was a question he wanted to ask Pinko, but knew it would alert him, best play dumb and compliant, a member of the team just doing his job.

Sidney had to admit the constant mind games were getting him down, now that the brutal nature of the people he was involved in had been revealed; he was now living with a measure of fear and apprehension. Frank and Bob seemed to revel in it, but he found it difficult, mainly because Penelope was involved, he felt responsible, she was a planning officer not a secret agent, but it seemed to him, she did think like one. He decided to concentrate on the preparation work for the opening ceremony.

CHAPTER 25
HEAD DOWN

The first couple of weeks were sorting out a myriad of loose ends, there must be no mistake, too many people were reliant upon a satisfactory completion, not least himself. Though how the discovery of the underground vaults would impact things was anyone's guess, at least this should shift the focus from him.

In the back of Sidney's mind was the hidden agenda of Goth Enactments and the feeling that he should be doing something about it. His growing reliance on Frank and Bob as the professionals was, he felt, unhealthy. He would normally take the initiative when dealing with situations like this, but this was something out of the ordinary.

Designing and building a wooden siege machine for a master criminal as a weapon of mass destruction; to fall in love with a beautiful girl; to be involved with agents of the government and find a long-lost Saxon king's burial chamber, was what one might say living life to the full. Sidney might argue and say: this was living life on the edge, the edge of a nervous breakdown.

To add to the ever-increasing pressure, Penelope had invited him to meet her mother that evening, only for supper she said. Nevertheless, he dressed immaculately, it was instinctive, a façade to cover any insecurity that may show. It was a plus that Penelope liked him well dressed, it was also a plus that her mother liked him as well. He wondered where her father was but didn't want to enquire. It was a nice evening and informative, it was obvious that her mother was reliant upon Penelope in many ways, it was a nice family atmosphere, something he missed.

The next day he decided to ask Frank what Penelope and himself should be doing, time was moving on and they were no nearer to solving the mystery. Frank was diplomatic, but the many words he used conveyed a simple message. Sidney was to keep his head down, focus on work, talk to no one and wait, but that didn't really help, he was left feeling like a fidgety schoolboy.

CHAPTER 26
UNVEILING

The unveiling, or to be precise, the removal of the sheeted scaffolding over the war machine, was not ceremonial. It took four days to dismantle and caused a lot of public interest. The images on Facebook went worldwide. The war machine emerged from its hibernation with dignity, like a gigantic chrysalis entering in a world of sunshine and admiring onlookers. Gossamer wings it did not have, but a shimmering, cascading layer of colourful shields it did, a coat of many colours. It stood immobile, passive, but gave the impression of a thing ready for violent action, it looked as though it were full of hidden energy—a mighty power ready to be unleashed.

The public were ecstatic, but at the same time humbled and in awe of this towering, powerful edifice. It was an image of medieval power at its zenith. The following media frenzy took a turn for the worse when Herbie, eager to ride on a wave of fame and possible notoriety, declared he was going to breed alpacas, out of respect for his client. People who knew him, knew of course that he didn't like animals. Words are cheap, they said, breeding alpacas isn't.

Sidney's daily workload became intense. This gave him a sense of isolation from the underlying reality, the knowledge of the evil intentions and machinations of his employer, Goth Enactment Ltd which was growing ever stronger. It was the awful feeling of being used, being out of control. It was obvious, when trying to look at the bigger picture, that Pinko, so called, and the Chief Exec Jose were a couple of smooth operators, or were they? They were in control of spending just over three and half million pounds sterling, and they didn't even own the land their investment sat on, or in this case ran on.

He met Penelope after work, he was tired and it must have showed, Penelope was concerned. "You must take it easy Sidney, you cannot take the burden of the whole project alone, I'm here to help. And please let Frank and Bob worry about what to do, they're agents for the government, that's their job." He wanted to believe that, but knew his role was more crucial than just sitting back and letting events take their course.

He had been invited to her mother's for supper, they sat in the lounge, her mother was rattling cutlery in the kitchen. "It's like this." His voice hushed. "What we need to know is, who will be working and controlling the war machine when it's finished and fully operational?" He sipped his tea and looked Penelope in the eye. "What we should be saying to yourselves is, if the project is complete and we still don't know what it is for, we would have failed, that's as I see it, which is why we cannot let things just ride." The tiredness was getting worse and he must have sounded as though he was having a whinge.

"I still feel Frank and Bob have a responsibility," she said, "We must trust them; I believe they know more than we think. The whole thing feels quite evil to me and I don't want you to go it alone."

CHAPTER 27
LEGAL

Nick Tweed wanted to see Penelope and Sidney again, this time there would be no Pinko. "I have a problem," he said, asking them to sit. Penelope thought it chilly with the air conditioning on, but better that than too hot. "The problem is a legal one." He put a copy of an ordinance survey sheet on the table, they could see it covered the church and castle and the land in between. Sidney had seen it before; he had built his model from it.

"Now the problem is this: we know the extent of the underground vaults or under croft now, it has been measured, it covers an area of approximately twenty thousand square feet, the size of an out-of-town supermarket. If we look at the plan, I have had this marked up." He indicated the area coloured up.

"This medieval underground structure appears to be in three ownerships, that is as far as the plan is concerned. In the first part: Historic England with the grounds of Battle-Cry Castle. The second part: The Church Commissioners, with the grounds to the Church and the third part: Cry City Council have a road running down the middle." The areas were coloured; Sidney could see the ramp position.

Nicks voice had a resigned tone. "My legal department have been working on this, trying to unravel it all, it is by no means simple. And to add to the complexity, Herbert Strange is claiming ancient rights of ownership of the vaults as the legal owner of the access from Castle Ditch House." He paused for them to digest. Sidney was wondering what the problem was, he could think of quite a few, not least the legal arguments that would ensue.

Nick Tweed, as head of planning, had experienced quite a few dramas in his time, but not of this messy magnitude. He placed on the table a collection of documents. "These are copies of the deeds to Castle Ditch House, they date back to 1575 AD." He spread them out. "Now, coming to the problem I mentioned." He chose one of the documents, it was coloured. "This is the most current and is dated 1886 AD, I have highlighted the parts I want you to read."

Penelope and Sidney looked at the plans, they were copies, but they could see the age. "This is what I want you to see," said Nick, pointing to the top of the plan.

Penelope read it out loud. "Castle Ditch House, formally Dyke House, was built by the order of King James for the sole purpose of keeping and affording access in perpetuity to the royal burial chamber of the Saxon king... This is by Royal Decree—gosh," gasped Penelope. "And it's signed by the King." Her voice breathless.

"Sorry to put a damper on things, but we now come to the problem." Nick said it with a touch of irony in his voice. "Goth Enactments are claiming three point five million pounds compensation for denying them access over the full length of the ramp which goes over the portion of land the vaulted under-croft is under."

"What?" echoed Penelope and Sidney. "That is scandalous—disgusting," Sidney blurted out. "They are crooks, the lot of them, and to think I work for them." He wanted to say more, but thought better of it, Frank wouldn't have approved.

Nick in a consolatory tone explained. "I know this is upsetting, but I have the Chief Executive of Cry Council on my back, he is beside himself with anger, a three point five-million-pound claim against the council will not be tolerated—his words." Sidney could see he was under pressure.

"Sidney, I am sorry to put you in this position, but our Chief Exec would like you to be a mediator and communicate with your Chief Exec." Sidney's heart sank, the thought of dealing with Jose, the thick necked Peruvian thug, filled him with dread, but the words that came out of his mouth belied his misgivings. "Would you like me to discuss his claim with him, happy to do so if you wish."

Nick Tweed looked relieved. "Good, good, that would be ideal, I must say it would be so helpful. Perhaps you could report back on the outcome, this is most urgent and the most delicate of tasks, I can't thank you enough." Sidney had the funny feeling that he had committed himself to a course of events that could only end up in a downward spiral. He might have avoided it if Penelope hadn't been there, but a manly stance it had to be.

CHAPTER 28
LONDON

Pinko was in a buoyant mood when Sidney approached him. "Well now," he said, "so, the council have asked you to have a chat with Mr Jose, that's interesting. That tells me that they are worried, presumably they have asked you to be a negotiator?"

Sidney hesitated, he was not sure if negotiator was the right term, it was simply a discussion. "Perhaps if I could meet with Mr Jose, maybe he could advise, three and a half million pounds is a lot of money."

A thought had come to Sidney in the early hours, were their demands opportunistic, taking advantage of the situation, or was it leading to further planning negotiations, either way, meeting Jose was the only way to find out. Pinko said Mr Jose wanted to see him in their London office, he would discuss matters there.

This suited Sidney, he welcomed a break from the intense activity on site and sadly from Cry City itself. Things were getting personal and Bob was only there nights. He went by train and then tube, he walked to Bryanston Square W1. Jose's office, it transpired, occupied the whole of one tall, Georgian, terraced house, it had an abundance of creamy white panelling, shutters and heavily corniced ceilings, it was impressive.

A mousey middle-aged woman ushered him into Mr Jose's office. The man sat impassively; a formidably wide, squat figure, behind an even wider mahogany desk. He was more intimidating than when he first met him, maybe it was the room? It was more two rooms, the dividing doors were open creating an enormous space, the full depth of the building, some ten metres or so. The wall on one side was covered in bookshelves.

Mr Jose stood up. "Please take a seat." There was a lone chair placed central to the massive desk, Sidney thanked him and was conscious that they were meeting once again with no physical contact. "I asked to see you Sidney, may I call you Sidney?" He continued without waiting for a reply. "I want you to know that I appreciate your willingness to help us in the negotiations with Cry Council for the compensation claim. Mr Tweed has been most helpful and thinks highly of you."

Sidney's uncomfortable feeling increased. Jose's words were reasonable, but his tone of voice had subliminal, menacing undertones. The man was his boss, yet somehow conveyed the impression that he was his executioner. He attempted to show his willingness that Jose had spoken of. "Thank you, I have lived in Cry City all my life and in working for Herbert Strange I have come to know the council staff and members well, so happy to help." He spoke calmly with measured tones, he waited.

Jose looked coldly at Sidney. "In my country we have our own way of negotiating." His cruel lips puckered unpleasantly, and his glittering eyes disappeared into the folds of his fleshy face, Sidney thought he may have smiled.

Sidney decided to be bold, it might change the man's attitude. "I know the council well and my view is, they will close ranks, hide behind a wall of legalise and slow things down, the usual lawyer's tactic to gain thinking time. I am not being negative, just realistic."

Jose's eyes widened at this and he sat back a little in his plush leather chair. "Are you saying the four million pounds compensation we are claiming will not be paid?" Sidney was taken aback; Nick had shown him the claim and it was three point five million.

"Well Mr Jose, firstly, if the principle is agreed, only then can the amount be agreed." Sidney had avoided talking about figures in the hope that common sense would prevail.

Jose's response however was curt. "Principle you say," his tone raised. "Let me tell you, young man, I am a man of principles and I can assure you that denying me my rights is a matter of principle, and I will take action if I am not supported in my reasonable requests and my legal team will be instructed, if you could convey that to Mr Tweed's advisors I would be obliged." The audience with the Chief Executive of Goth Enactments Ltd was terminated.

Sidney felt he had accomplished nothing, but at least he could make a report out. It was obvious he was being used as a messenger. He was on the phone most of the journey back, he felt drained and made his excuses to Penelope and went straight home.

CHAPTER 29
POLITICAL

The wind of change; Penelope felt emotionally stirred. The impact of discovering that there were ancient vaults under the city brought a wave of excitement, but she knew that this was bound to trigger off a wave of controlling issues and sadly, greed. The public, however, were relatively unaffected by the politics and were enjoying the prospect of another important historic venue. Sadly, this was not so for her and Sidney, things were not the same, and the signs were there that indicated, they could be getting worse.

Sidney was enmeshed in getting the war machine visitor friendly. He said, whilst there was still lots to do inside the office accommodation, the sling arm was fully operational and ready to use. It was the electrical services that needed finishing off. Pinko said this wouldn't hold things up, the electricians could carry on working inside, which would affect no one.

It all sounded so reasonable to Penelope, she almost forgot the political row that was brewing. The first of the four landowners affected by the vaulted under croft had protested, excluding Herbie who was making his own claim. It was Historic England; Jasper Thorndyke was in full flight; his eloquent emails were pitched at gaining control, rather than diplomatic negotiations. He rarely got what he wanted, most people ignored him and sometimes that included the council's solicitors.

Jasper did have a strong case however, or so he said, because of the burial vault of the Saxon king. Herbie's reaction to that, which was tinged with not a little measure of sarcasm. "You will find the burial vault outside of the land owned by Historic England." Jasper did not respond; silence is golden—his own golden rule when losing.

Penelope found this constant manoeuvring and bickering tiresome. However, she could see it brewing into a serious conflict, no good would come of it. Her job as senior planning officer was to avoid conflict with applicants, the public and site owners, not always one and the same person. The prime motivation for development was money, an increase in site value the key to success. With Jasper it was different, he wanted fame.

CHAPTER 30
JASPER

The day started with a measure of normality; Sidney was endeavouring to maintain equilibrium in the power struggle going on. His workload helped; Pinko was pushing him hard and he had little time to puzzle over what evil complications were manifesting in the background, and who was doing what.

Penelope turned up mid-morning, Sidney was relieved to see her. "Ha! My little ray of sunshine." His smile faded at the look on her face, it was white with distress. "What's the matter Penelope?" he walked over to her, his heart beating fast.

"It's Jasper." Her voice trembled. "He's dead; the police are dealing with it." She sat down on the nearest chair and fumbled with her bag, he thought she might want a tissue, he handed her a box. "Thank you." Her hands were shaking; he wondered what to say, so he asked gently. "Police involved! what happened to him?"

"They say its murder; he was found in the vaults at Herbie's, who is in a bit of a state, he found him. "Sidney waited, he wanted to question her, but thought it best for her to explain in her own time. "Well apparently," she sniffed, "Herbie left him for the morning at Castle Ditch House to explore the vaults, he was supposed to switch off the lights and put the key through the letter box when he had finished.

When Herbie arrived later the place was still open and the lights on down in the vaulted under croft. When he got down there, he found Jasper spread-eagled on his back, laying on the entrance stone to the vault of the Saxon ing." She paused and blew her nose. "That's all I know, Herbie told Nick and Nick told me the little he knew, it was in the strictest confidence and now I am telling you, I feel guilty about that, but I needed to talk to someone, there's so much going on and my mother is no good at comforting."

Sidney took the hint and pulled a chair next to her and put his arm around her shoulders. "I am here, you're safe with me." Sidney found the story difficult to take in, he could understand Jasper being there, it was his job. He couldn't imagine someone following him in, so it could have been someone he knew or someone they both knew.

"Look, I'll make us a drink, I want to help if I can, not sure what though, I could ring Herbie of course, but that might be seen as a lack of tact." Penelope looked relieved; he could see she felt comforted. He felt protective towards her and she had known Jasper a long time. Sidney only knew him by reputation, but there were qualities he had that were less then admirable. He could not imagine the man having many friends.

CHAPTER 31
MATTHIAS

Matthias Oldham, as conservation officer for Cry City Council took his custodial duties seriously and was quietly nursing, with considerable care and tact, the historic buildings within the borough and under his jurisdiction. The duties of his quiet, methodical working life were only ever disturbed by disgruntled historic property owners, who wanted to do something that did not meet with, or conform to, the regulations. It was mostly a matter of taste, and his was impeccable.

He had just returned from a month's holiday in Rome, a place full of history and romance, his four children had made it difficult for him to relax and he was glad to get back. He was wading through the backlog of emails, when he came across one from Penelope Pride, with a plan attached.

He was shocked, he read it three times before he could grasp it. Jasper Thorndyke had been found murdered in a newly discovered maze of vaults and tunnels in the grounds of Battle-Cry Castle and the church. As he looked at the plan, the shock of death evaporated at the thought of this exciting discovery.

He spoke with Penelope on the phone and was frustrated to hear that he would be denied access to this incredible find. It was now a crime scene and sealed off. Exciting things always happen when I am on holiday, was his forlorn moan.

CHAPTER 32
INSPECTOR BUCK

The following three days seemed to drag, Penelope tried to concentrate on work, but gossip in the council offices was rife! It was obvious that Herbie had been less than discreet, and lurid details of his gruesome find were on everyone's lips. The most startling of which was the screwed-up copy email he had found stuffed in Jasper's mouth. He refused to divulge its contents but said the police would know what to do.

Penelope had worked closely with Jasper on a few historic buildings and knew him to be honest, but self-centred and extremely irritating. Nick asked to see her again; the last time was the news of Jasper's death; what this time. She felt apprehensive; there may be further developments.

As she climbed the stairs, Nick's office was two floors above hers, she felt breathless with anxiety. He was waiting for her, he showed her into his small conference room, there was a man sitting there. As he stood up, she noticed he was tall, heavily built and formally dressed. "I would like you to meet Inspector Buck, Penelope he is investigating Jasper Thorndyke's tragic death. He is a policeman."

The man looked at her kindly, which was a relief. She shook hands and took the seat offered. There was an uncomfortable silence, the inspector spoke first. "Thank you for seeing me Miss Pride, as you may be aware, I know Mr Tweed has informed you of it. I am investigating the death of a Mr Japer Thorndyke, I believe you knew him." He waited for her to reply.

"I knew him reasonably well, we worked together on projects, though not here, he worked for Historic England." Buck pulled out a notebook.

"Did you?" he paused, opening it. "Did you meet him at the vaults last week—let's see, yes, Wednesday?"

He seemed a relaxed sort and she felt more at ease now. "Yes, there was a group of us," her voice gaining strength. "Nick was helping Herbert Strange to conduct a tour for the planning committee of the medieval vaults. Jasper was there as an advisor on historic buildings." She paused unsure of what to say next; Buck consulted his notebook.

"I understand that Mr Thorndyke—Jasper, was ill at ease, frightened perhaps."

She felt her face redden. "Well perhaps he was a bit nervous, we all were. It's a creepy place and we were all huddled together; it was very dark."

She had hoped this would satisfy him, but no. "Tell me," his voice had a steely edge to it, "what was your opinion of Mr Thorndyke, from a professional perspective?" She felt trapped; Jasper had been a pompous, arrogant, self-centred bore.

"He could be difficult," she replied. "But then, he was passionate about buildings and appeared quite straightforward in his approach to work." She felt she had batted that back quite well, but her newfound confidence was about to take another blow.

"Did you have any disagreements," She felt hot again, many a time she had arguments with Jasper, mainly because he seemed to revel in it. So, did that make her a murderer? I must be prudent she thought, this could be a trick question.

"He had his funny ways, but we always got the job done." She looked pleadingly at Nick, he smiled and looked at Inspector Buck.

"Thank you, Miss Pride, most helpful."

Penelope was glad to escape, she felt like a criminal. Sidney suggested afterwards that they meet to discuss events, particularly now that Herbie had spread the word.

CHAPTER 33
FORCES

For Sidney, the murder of Jasper was a wake-up call. It helped him focus on the people and organisations involved, and their individual agendas. He found it helped to note down the six organisations or groups and one character that was directly involved. To clear his mind, he decided to write down the eight-key people and their organisations.

Dame Nancy Hard-Castle OBE: Chair of Planning Committee, Cry City Council. A formidable woman who had influence over the members.

Jasper Thorndyke, deceased: Inspector for Historic England, no influence now, but left a legacy of confusion and fear.

Harold Flint: Vicar of Cry City Church, a gentle soul who only wanted peace not war, so the war machine was not top of his agenda.

Tony Lane: Cry City Council roads department, he denied any knowledge of a tomb under his road, before my time, he said.

Herbert Strange: owner of Castle Ditch House, possession is nine tenths of the law, his claim, not the lawyer acting for him.

Goth Enactments: a legal right to use a strip of land, over the discovered vaults, for the use of their siege machine.

Inspector Buck: Cry City Police Department, an enigma,

currently unsure of his astuteness.

Captain Frank Miles: SAS, who had taken an interest from the start, role: probably to protect the governments interests.

Having jotted down the headings, he thought it a good idea to talk through the situation with Penelope, she was very good with facts. It might also help the police catch the murderer. She was enthusiastic about that and they met at Don's for coffee. "Do you think Inspector Buck will be doing something like us Sidney? We could set up a pin-board in your flat and pin notes on it.

Sidney was relieved that she appeared to have got over the shock of Jasper's death. "Great idea, I will get one; you can see from my list," he handed her a copy, "that three parties have part legal ownership and two have legal rights of way to or over the ground." Penelope studied the list then said.

"Do you think the Crown Estates will have a possible interest, with a king buried in the vaults? Sorry to complicate things, but better consider it." She smiled, but it was mischievous.

"That's a good point, I shall add that to the list," he said, "It could count in our favour."

They sipped their drinks, silent for a few moments. Sidney looked at his list again. "My feeling is that among this list, or amongst all the personalities we know, and are involved is our killer. I believe the planning application and the approval triggered off Jasper's tragic death. But why? That is the mystery."

Penelope looked impressed. "I think you sound like a policeman, Sidney. There is one thing thought that keeps nagging at me, what did the email say that was stuffed in Jasper's mouth? She shuddered as she said it, she continued.

"I did hear in the office that Herbie said it was one of Jasper's special emails to the Cry City Council legal department, he wanted them to eat their words."

Her attempt at a joke was admirable thought Sidney, he smiled encouragement. "The email was full of accusations, but nobody knows what they were, Herbie won't say. Another rumour was it involved two of the councillors on the planning committee."

Sidney was pleased, information was flowing between them and a picture was beginning to take shape. His office on site near the war machine wasn't safe, his suspicions again, but he did suspect it was bugged. He emailed Frank and Bob a resume of his meeting with Penelope, it sounded formal, but he had a strong feeling that collecting information was not going to be easy. Frank responded first, he telephoned later in the day.

"We are aware of the current situation Sidney, and Bob has been keeping me informed. I am talking to Inspector Buck and I am now fully in the picture." Sidney thought he sounded like a man under stress. "I think Sidney, that you and Penelope need to be careful, do not leave Penelope alone. I can tell you that the discovery of the medieval vaults has upset the plans of someone, what and who, we don't know yet, but we are working on it."

Sidney got no encouragement from the call, quite the reverse. Now he was worried about Penelope, how could he protect her? and why did Frank make a point about protecting her? As Bob was now a regular nightly visitor, he thought he would ask him, he might shed some light on the matter. He had sensed Frank's reticence to give him the full picture, he felt nervous; things, it would seem, were becoming dangerous.

He did not feel close to the situation as before. Events were leaving him behind; rapidly changing attitudes of people and the organisations they worked for was unsettling and unpredictable. Being in the field, so to speak, Bob was more available to speak to, and easier to meet up with. That aside, Sidney was wondering if they, being Frank and Bob, were keeping him in the dark a little, playing him along. After all it was them that approached him.

The latest dialogue with them did not fill him full of confidence. It seemed to him that he had entered the murky world of spies uninvited and would need to fend for himself. Penelope seemed better equipped to cope, she was attractive and lifted the spirits of all she was with by her bubbly personality.

And what did he have? A head full of knowledge and a suspicious nature, which may be ideal for espionage activities but not for forming bonds of friendship and trust. The murder of Jasper, for some, caused confusion and fear, for others a subliminal sense of excitement—the fight or flight syndrome. Nature has a way of selecting those for fighting and when that happens, it's usually surprising.

CHAPTER 34
PUBLIC DISPLAY

The day had arrived for the public to view the war machine, it could not be put off, though Sidney thought it should have been out or respect for Jasper. Mr Jose was adamant, his investment must be protected, and the awful murder had happened underground anyway, so, out of sight out of mind, those were his words. Penelope appalled at the man's insensitivity; she said would help Sidney on the day, which was now. She could see he was stressed. "It's the workers inside," he said, "They wanted space and be left alone, lots of expensive equipment to install, that was what they moaned about, noise would be a distraction."

The public arrived at nine a.m. prompt, the queuing snacked its way back to the High Street. There was a real buzz in the air. Sidney had arranged for an external viewing platform to be erected complete with a staircase, an open scaffolded tower. This would enable the public to see the top of the war machine at close quarters and appreciate the power the sling arm possessed. It would also compensate for the lack of access to the inside. Sidney was trying to keep everyone happy, it seemed to be working and he was just starting to relax.

It happened at about mid-day. It was a small noise, but sharp and piercing. Sidney was standing guard by the door to the offices with Penelope, he looked up towards the sound, it appeared to come from the sling arm. It took a few moments for Sidney to realise that the noise was in fact a scream. There was a silence as the public stopped and looked, like him towards the sound. The silence was eerie, as though everyone was waiting for an encore. There was another scream, unmistakable this time, it was a woman in distress. Then came her heart rending cries and shouts for help.

"Penelope," cried Sidney. "Look its Rose Archer, she's right at the top of the machine, do you see? Its where the sling arm is hinged; I can see her head."

Penelope grabbed Sidney's arm. "How did she get right up there?" her voice anxious.

Sidney replied. "There are men working in there, they may be able to help her, I should have a number." He scrolled his mobile phone.

The public were now getting animated and crowding together for a better look. Sidney got through; it was one of the electricians. "You need to come up here Sidney." He gasped his voice full of fear. "Someone has been killed, I don't know if it's an accident or not, we are trying to help." He cut the phone off. Sidney's heart sank, then started to thump; another death, was it the same method and murder again.

"I would like you to stay here Penelope, by the door—please and don't let anyone in." He was through the door and gone in a stride.

Sidney had climbed the spiral oak staircase many times, but never at speed. He instinctively stayed near the centre, less travel distance. He met no one on the way up. It was three flights to the fourth-floor level, and he arrived breathless. The four men were standing over a body, Daphne Darling was kneeling over it and sobbing, it was Bobby Bowman. He was laying on his back, he looked peaceful as though he was sleeping. "Someone shot him in the chest." It was one of the electricians, he pointed to a short piece of wood that was sticking out of his chest. "I think it's a bolt from a crossbow, you can just see the flight, it went in deep. He must have died quickly; I am a first aider and could do nothing." Daphne increased her sobbing at that harsh statement of fact.

Sidney felt duty bound to take control. "Daphne," he gently took her arm, "shall we go down now and let the medical team do their job, there's nothing more you can do here."

The ambulance siren sounded outside. She was still sobbing as he helped her down the spiral stair—keeping in front for support. Penelope was waiting at the bottom. "I have called the police; they had a message already and are on their way." She spoke softly out of respect to Daphne, but she was in such a state of shock, she appeared oblivious.

"Will you be OK here? I need to go up again." Penelope nodded; she had her arm around Daphne. He felt a need to inspect the body again and ask some more questions. Two deaths in one week was no coincidence. The four men were standing away from the body, obviously not sure what to do. "May I suggest you stay and wait for the police on the next level down, the police will not be impressed with us contaminating the crime scene." He watched them go down and took photos on his phone before following them. Billy Bowman looked as though he was resting, there was little blood.

"We reckon the shot came from just below the church spire. There's a parapet, whoever it was must have aimed from there. Billy was standing in the open on the small maintenance platform on the roof, the one under the hinged part of the sling arm. When he was hit, he fell backwards down the hatch to the floor below." The man was clearly shaken.

Sidney thanked him saying, "The police will be here soon." He didn't know what else to say, they waited in silence, then they heard men's voices, which grew louder as they approached the top. A large figure emerged, it was Inspector Buck and one of his officers.

Sidney moved forward to greet him, but he wasn't quick enough. "Ah! Mr Picket, we meet again. Where is the deceased?" Sidney pointed up. The inspector carried on up the spiral stair to the fourth floor followed by his officer. Sidney followed close behind, Buck didn't say otherwise. He stood back while the inspector studied the body. "Hum!" Buck murmured. "A medieval mace and now a crossbow." Sidney was startled, so Jasper was killed with a mace, how did they know that?

The general hubbub of milling crowds had died to a silence—a deathly silence. Sidney felt he needed to talk to Frank or Bob, why didn't they tell him about the mace? They must have known; he then became anxious about Penelope, he desperately wanted to get down to see if she was OK. But at the same time didn't want to miss anything Buck might say, Penelope won.

Harold Flint, the vicar of Cry City church was of a pious, soft personality and violence was abhorrent to him and a violation to his peaceful and meaningful relationship with God. It was therefore understandable that he was mortified that a missile of death had been fired from the roof of his church, a place of sanctuary and peace for the persecuted. The inspector had asked Sidney to take him to meet Flint.

The question Inspector Buck had for the Rev Flint was, "Who has authority to gain access to the roof, Reverend, and do you keep a record of maintenance activities and such like?"

The vicar looked defensive. "It's the verger's job." Was his prompt reply, meaning, nothing to do with him. Confronted by tall, sturdily built Buck, Flint was like a rabbit in the headlights of a car. The inspector seemed satisfied with what information he had gained and left. Sidney made a polite exit minutes later, after saying how sorry he was for this sad event to Flint.

It was Penelope who hit on a possible explanation, though bizarre to the extreme. "I think the killer has a macabre plan, which he is executing, please excuse the pun, in the elimination of members of the planning committee. He is inspired by the victim's names and status, rather than anything else. Billy Bowman, killed with a crossbow and Jasper Thorndyke, killed with a genuine fifteenth century medieval mace, a coincidence, highly unlikely."

"I can see that," said Sidney. "What we need to concern ourselves with now, is, who's next."

He looked at Penelope, she grimaced. "I have another thought," she said, "it's along the lines we spoke of before, is the targeting aimed at committee members and others who supported the planning application for the war machine? There could be a protester that's gone rogue.

CHAPTER 35
SPEAR

Penelope couldn't get it out of her head that names were important to the killer, maybe he wanted to encourage the police to believe they were when really there was another agenda. She found it difficult to stay focused, the media was having a field day. Mock medieval battle, the papers proclaimed, Ancient Mace fight ends in Death, and Arrows of misfortune for War Machine. Etc.

The third incident was dramatic, but not fatal. In hindsight, it should have been expected and precautions taken, but sadly not so, complacency set in and with it a measure of unbelief. Jack Spear was in the open and relaxing among friends. It was Wanda Longstaff who was there and relayed the story to Penelope.

"Apparently, and this is the incredible part, someone threw a spear over twenty metres and hit Jack, nearly fair and square, fortunately not square enough. Jack was sitting at a table having refreshments in the grounds of Battle-Cry Castle. The table had a parasol supported by a thin white pole, and would you believe it the spear, speared the pole, which was directly in line with the flight path to Jack's chest. Well, it cut the pole in half, was deflected and hit and gashed Jack's shoulder to the bone. He is now in hospital, but alive." She ended her account with a Churchillian style statement. "This is real war with real weapons."

Inspector Francis Buck was trying to contain the situation, escalating violence between so called sophisticated people was bewildering. This was getting out of hand. In one way he was annoyed that these Frank and Bob characters from London were involved, he was told one of them was ex SAS. He was relaying his concerns to Penelope; he had realised early on that she and Sidney Picket had the ear of the two government men. He thought Sidney was too strong and decided to talk to Penelope.

Penelope thought that Frank was the clever one and she guessed the inspector thought so as well. Bob, she realised now was the physical part of the team, he did look tough. Frank had called a meeting, it would be at the Cry City Council offices in the Ccommittee room, his secretary had sent out invites to all those summoned. It looked a serious matter, thought Penelope, but then death was serious.

Frank outranked Inspector Buck and so did Bob, whose SAS status had filtered through. The people called to the meeting, were all those who had attended the planning meeting that determined the permission of the war machine. Those not attending were: Jasper Thorndyke, deceased; Billy Bowman, deceased; and Jack Spear, almost deceased. Daphne Darling was in a mess and pleaded compassionate leave.

Dame Nancy Hard-Castle OBE was secretly pleased that Jasper was gone and had, unfortunately, expressed this to someone in private. She knew he would never let her misdemeanour be forgotten.

Digby Pike was now standing in for Billy Bowman, though he felt uncomfortable being in a dead man's shoes. Henry Odd said he would be happy to help fill the space of Jack Spear.

The committee room was silent, they all waited for the new chairman. "My name is Frank Miles and my colleague here is Bob Bloom." He turned to Bob who sat impassive. All there were reasonably relaxed and sort of comfortable. Frank, with his polite hosting had cleverly given the impression of a fussing hen collecting his chicks under his wings. Penelope was impressed, he was clearly used to heavy meetings and this looked like being one.

It was a disarming act, engineered to cohere them into the right frame of mind, but in a kindly fashion. Penelope thought at first it was because of the deaths, but she soon realised otherwise.

They all sat in their normal seats, except Dame Nancy Hard- Castle OBE, she was not in the Chair. Frank Miles had taken her place, so she sat in Billy Bowman's seat. Things started at a pace. Frank immediately asserted his authority; gone was his soft, diplomatic demeanour.

He picked Dame Hard-Castle first. "I can see," he said glaring around at the assembly until his eyes rested upon the dame, "from the file I have in front of me, that it is recorded that Dame Hard-Castle had made a complaint against the deceased Jasper Thorndyke, which the deceased claimed were spurious. And the consequences were, he was furious. Now what is your recollection of this event Dame Hard-Castle?"

They all looked at the dame, who visible blanched at the sound of her name. Penelope thought she looked smaller. "I made a mistake," she said in a low voice. "I made a statement about it." She looked down at her hands.

"Quite-quite," said Frank. "But my question is, what is your recollection. You do see that I am concerned about the animosity between yourself and Jasper Thorndyke and now one of you is dead—murdered. Please answer my question."

Penelope glanced at Sidney, his face was expressionless, but she felt sure he was enjoying the proceedings. Nick Tweed looked alert and obviously keen to know all the facts. Inspector Buck was not so alert, his thunder had been taken away.

Dame Nancy Hard-Castle OBE was now on the receiving end of an experienced and tough interrogator. A new chairperson with a mission. All could see that the dame was crumbling, some, Penelope knew would be pleased. The bond, the comradery of a united committee, now gone. Sarcastic tomfoolery, the glue that held them together, was now unstuck.

"I am sorry," the dame's voice now a whimper. "I said it was a mistake, Jasper took it personally, he was nasty to me." She got a tissue out and put it to her nose, they all felt sure she was going to cover her face, but she blinked and carried on. "He said he would report me for unprofessional conduct." She gasped. "But I didn't kill him—you must believe me." She started to weep at this point, there was a silence.

Penelope wondered what Frank would do, she felt sure he had attacked her, first in order to soften up her resistance and any resistance in the other committee members. "Thank you, thank you." It was a dismissal, Dame Hard-Castle quietly sniffled. Frank Miles continued with boldness.

"Now Billy Bowman and Daphne Darling are unable to attend, one as you know, is dead and Daphne Darling is recovering from shock at home, with her husband Mr Darling." He stopped, reflected. "I should say at this point, and I am aware that this is common knowledge, that Daphne and Billy were having an affair. Mr Darling is disabled, so he can be ruled out as the killer." He took a sip of water. "Jack Spear is not here." The ghost of a smile flickered across his face at the rhyming rhythm. "It is a miracle he survived by all accounts and whoever threw the spear must have been a strong athletic type, we think it was a man, but a female cannot be ruled out. The throwing distance was over twenty metres and deadly accurate, though not with the deadly consequences required—thank God.

Frank paused and shuffled the papers in front of him. Penelope was impressed, he obviously had done this sort of thing before. He continued, "Ladies and gentlemen, you now have a precis of the three disturbing events and what I would like to do next, is to ask each of you to give a brief statement of your knowledge of these three happenings, whether you were personally involved or not. And for the record, this meeting is being recorded, so no need to keep notes, only if you wish." He looked around at them all. "I will start on my left and go around clockwise."

It was a long and tedious process, there were twelve testimonies to hear and many questions to be asked and answered. It dawned on Penelope halfway through that maybe Frank wanted all their voices recorded. That way each audible testimony could then be analysed, to find any faults and fear inflections. In one sense, the group would have a feeling of comfort being together and knowing each other, guards would be down, and if the killer was among them her or she might make a mistake. She thought Bob would be kept busy.

CHAPTER 36
ARCHER

It was Herbie who knew Rose Archer best, they used to play squash sometimes in the local club, with other members of the committee. It was his little bit of networking, until increased weight restricted his movements.

Rose was a single girl and as swift and agile as an Ibex. Herbie found her fun to be with, but only on a social level, in any other scenario she would be classed as bossy. It was the major flaw that marred her otherwise jolly disposition. It was unfortunate, but there was nothing anyone could do about it, or wanted to.

It was six days after the Jack Spear attack that Rose Archer was targeted. She had driven to the squash club, it was safe there and she would be among friends, people she knew. Dressed in white with a short skirt, she made an attractive sight. She was handsome, in a Nordic way, her mother came from Spitzbergen. In her defence, Herbie thought she was a generous person, though did admit to close friends that he suspected her generosity was for personal gain.

The squash courts were busy, the sounds of pained grunts and squeaky shoes filled the air. Rose Archer was being stalked. The attack when it came was swift, unexpected and terminal. Rose Archer was dead before she hit the polished beech floor. The missile transpired to be an early musket ball, large, about thirty centimetres in diameter. It was fired down from the viewing platform overlooking the court she was playing in.

It had apparently happened when she stopped for a refreshment. The musket ball had been fired from above using some sort of catapult, it hit her on top of the head. There was no blood and it took a while for members to discover what the problem was, they thought she had been overdoing it.

Inspector Buck was frustrated again, he couldn't find any clues that would lead to a suspect. Frank called a meeting, but this time just the four of them, Penelope, Sidney, Bob and himself. "I have Inspector Buck's report on this latest murder." Frank placed a document on the table; they had met at Sidney's flat, it was close to the site and less public.

"This makes a dent in the number of committee members," said Bob. "Four down and nine do go." There was an awkward silence.

"Sorry," said Penelope, "don't you mean, three down and ten to go, Jasper was not on the committee and neither am I." Her voice showed her frustration and there was fear. She could be a target and so could Sidney.

It was Frank who eased the tension. "Please forgive us, both of you, I need to tell you that Bob and I are ex SAS and fatalities have been part of our daily life. Sadly, we are hardened to death. You are both at risk, that is why we are here now. The killer would have identified both Bob and I as their enemy and probably know our connection with you both and may take action."

Bob looked around. "This is an ideal secure safe house Frank, do you both stay here?" Bob looked at them quizzically, his face bland.

Penelope blushed and said, "No, I live with my mother

about a mile away."

Bob smiled. "Maybe you should move in, it would be safer." It was Sidney's turn, he grinned sheepishly.

"Now," said Frank, "back to business, we need to analyse again, think of what it is the killer wants to achieve. Let's go back to the beginning and assume the vaulted under croft had never been found. We had a planning permission given and a war machine built, all was well, and plans were being made for the future festival activities—then the discovery of the vaults. The first death was in the vaults and this must have triggered off the others, but why?"

Sidney had a theory and felt now was the time to test it. "This may sound off the wall and influenced by my involvement, but it had occurred to me, that these deaths, this so-called persecution, is only a ploy to take attention away from the war machine, even Billy Bowman's death does that. People will be thinking of every conceivable cause for this brutal mayhem, but not the war machine. I hope this makes sense."

Frank looked intrigued. "What you are saying, Sidney, is Goth Enactments are behind it all," Bob responded. "That makes sense Frank, but very risky, we knew from the very first day that this company was iffy. The stakes must be high, but what are the stakes?"

CHAPTER 37
GRACE

It was Saturday mid-morning and the temperature in his top floor flat had been steadily rising. And so was his frustration, he had decided to make a mind map, a visual stimulation to help marshal the facts, to see if there was a pattern in the murders and the violence. To link Pinko and Jose to the church, Battle-Cry Castle and the vaults would be the breakthrough they needed.

He had done as Penelope had suggested and his pin-board was full of information. He stood back and studied it. Firstly, he had decided to look at the names of all the committee members, the killer seemed to be attracted to these. He let his eyes wander over the pin-board, and they settled on Gwendoline Grace. Gwendoline was originally from South Africa; she was a teacher and ran a local youth group.

There was something in the photo that attracted his eye, he looked closer. She was standing with Norman Keep, it looked like they were on a council summer outing trip together. The photo was cut from a Cry City Council magazine. There was something else, it was in the background and at a distance behind them, it was the distinctive and unmistakable, a red and white target for archery. "Gotcha." He said to himself out loud. So, there were possibly two murderers working together. No wonder the killings were varied, he looked closer at the photo again. Penelope had cut it out of the magazine so she should be able to find another one, there could be more information to be had.

Then something else, he could hardly contain his excitement. In Norman Keep's hand, but partly hidden behind his back was a bow, it could just be seen. Also, Gwendoline Grace had something over her shoulder and across her chest, it was the strap of an archer's quiver, he could just see the tips of the flights over her shoulder.

The first thing he did was take a photo on his phone, then emailed it to Penelope and copied Frank and Bob in. "I think we need to look into this," he wrote. "The coincidence is too strong to ignore, the two are both young and athletic types and by the looks of them physically capable of murder. It's alarming I know, but I have an uneasy feeling when I look at the both."

Penelope's reply was immediate. "They both have jobs linked with the council, I will make enquiries, well spotted Sidney, I will get back to you all."

Penelope's homework over the weekend then produced enough evidence to suggest that Sidney's theory could be right.

Frank phoned. "Well done Sidney, I think you have found something here, I have alerted Inspector Buck and he has arranged a surveillance team to track and follow Gwendoline and Norman. We must avoid another murder, so it's a worthwhile exercise, keeps them all on their toes. There could be a connection with them and Goth Enactments, just a thought."

CHAPTER 38
NORMAN

The murders had drawn attention away from the discovery of the medieval vaulted under-croft as a piece of important history. Jasper had drafted a report after his visit and whilst incomplete it did say—the main structure was early Norman, probably eleventh century, with some earlier structural elements, seemingly Saxon, which were in the area of the burial chamber. The vaulting generally indicates the possible existence or position of two earlier churches. Sidney was keen to know more, but realised mayhem and murders was not conducive to the quiet exploration of ancient history. Nevertheless, its discovery was of national importance and part of the journey they were both on.

Sidney had decided to visit the scene of the first crime again. Inspector Buck agreed, reluctantly Sidney thought, Herbie gave him the keys with a, "Look after yourself boy," comment. He decided to invite Penelope, she would be miffed if he didn't, but he was unsure if she would want to, she did.

It was a strange feeling going down the tunnel again, the lighting arrangement was the same. Herbie said he hadn't visited since the murder. The hustle of the High Street faded as they walked down the dimly lit vaulted under-croft. The silence was oppressive, as though the sound of the violence was still echoing in the atmosphere.

"Shall we look at Jasper's report," said Sidney. "It would

be helpful, I thought, to walk about and see what he saw, I might shed light on his thinking, he was extremely knowledgeable." Holding the report, they moved towards the scene of the violent deed. The police had left tape around the columns, but it was easy to view the floor and see the entrance stone to the burial vault, Sidney took a photo of the inscription.

"The blood stains are still there." His voice sombre. "It seems strange, yet symbolic somehow that a death should take place on top of a burial vault." As Penelope also took a photo on her phone he said. "The police report suggested the murder was executed in this fashion deliberately."

Penelope responded, "Perhaps it was engineered to look ritualistic, but really it was a brutal murder, pure and simple and this macabre display was just a smoke screen." They walked slowly on into the vaulted under-croft, keeping within the spread of the light bulbs.

"Doesn't it feel odd," Penelope said, "walking in a space that has been sealed for hundreds of years." Her voice hushed. Moments later she was nearly shouting. "Look—there." She was pointing her torch at the apex of an arch which was part of the external walling, there was a metal grilled high-level opening, they walked over to it. It was high up in the apex of an arch, it was about five metres from the ground to the apex and the bottom of the high-level opening was about three metres from the ground. The wall it was in faced Battle-Cry Castle.

"Amazing," exclaimed Sidney. "I wonder if there is a ladder in the house I would love to see inside. Let's go upstairs to see if we can find something, at least to stand on."

They made their way up to the ground floor and then up again and there they found the perfect thing, a short pair of decorator's steps. "Just the job," said Sidney enthusiastically. They carried it down to the vaults and took it in turns to look through the high-level grill and take photos.

What they saw took their breath away, it was another tunnel, but this time travelling towards the castle keep and it wasn't sloping upwards. "Incredible," gasped Sidney. "I wonder if this leads to the castle's basement, it looks crudely constructed to me, perhaps it was a siege tunnel, a means of attacking the castle."

They spent the rest of the day at Sidney's flat going over all the facts and theories. It had been an interesting day, from a historic point of view, but there was no eureka moment concerning the current situation.

CHAPTER 39
THE TRAP

Penelope had a plan, it was subliminal at first, but then surfaced growing into a definitive course of action. It was a plan to trap Gwendoline Grace and Norman Keep. The photos of them were damning evidence, but she felt they needed more. The idea was that Sidney and her would invite them for a meal at his flat, she would do the cooking and they would also invite Hazel Hope and Arnold Best, two of the committee members so far unaffected by the spate of violence.

"A dinner with friends at a time of crisis, seems an innocent pastime to me," declared Penelope and the guests agreed with that. Sidney was caught up in it all and Penelope left him to explain to Frank and Bob, she felt sure they would not be happy about it, but Sidney and her were at the coalface and sensitive to atmosphere, she also wanted to prove to Sidney that she was a competent cook.

The scene was set, Sidney had done a good job of setting the table and the two tall, thick candles were a nice touch. The whole thing was her idea and though she didn't have second thoughts about it, she was nervous. Sidney was relaxed and seemed to revel in this sort of pressure; he was immaculately dressed as usual.

The food was a success and Sidney looked impressed; she was pleased. It was Sidney who led the conversations. His seemingly innocent questions were revealing their personalities, helped by his manner of serving copious amounts of wine with the panache of a perfect host.

"I give Penelope all the credit and perhaps a little glory," he said chuckling and topping up everyone's glass. Amid this jollity and satiated hunger, he turned to Norman. "Norman, may I ask, what is your leisure activity—hobby?" He smiled disarmingly and continued, "Mine is sailing, I have a small boat moored just below the bridge, perhaps we could all go out for a sail sometime." He looked around the table beaming, as though he had forgotten his question to Norman.

"That would be nice," said Penelope, hearing for the first time he had a boat. Norman took the bait; his pride took over.

He was about forty, Sidney judged, strongly built, tall with no surplus fat. He had a steeliness about his manner and oozed self-confidence.

"I like archery," Norman said, his face showing an eagerness to share. Gwendoline gave him a nervous, worried sideways glance. Penelope had notice that Sidney had placed them side by side and facing him across the table. "I find the silence of archery exhilarating and when the arrow hits the target the small soft sound it makes is so satisfying, that is if you don't miss, which I do often." He laughed, but it was a laugh of arrogance, it was obvious he never missed.

Gwendoline looked uncomfortable; Penelope noticed a look of fear had flickered across her face. Sidney continued with his story. "I remember running aground once, I was left high and dry when the tide went out, it was pretty silent then I can tell you, though there was a bit of cursing going on." He grinned. "We had a long wait."

Norman responded. "I remember being in a tournament and my opponent decided to sulk, let me tell you, you can't afford to sulk at the level we were playing." He emphasised the we. At that moment Sidney decided he was one of the killers, if not the only one. Gwendoline was obviously the nervous type. But so, would I be, thought Sidney, if I was associated with Norman.

The rest of the evening was pleasant enough, particularly when he walked Penelope home.

CHAPTER 40
GRACE ABOUNDING

Sidney had been careful with the wine and was clear headed. It was seven forty-five when Bob phoned. "How did you get on last night" He sounded eager, no sign of disapproval that they had arranged something without discussing it with Frank.

"I am sure Norman Keep is our man," said Sidney. "Penelope, what should we do next?" He wanted to sound subservient.

Bob was the professional, his response was quick. "Wait—Frank says we wait, but take precautions, keep alert and anticipate trouble." His voice sounded firm. "Frank said there's something else that's brewing, but he will ring you later."

The rest of the morning was a bit flat he felt he should be doing more, but what? His role in the war machine project was not complete, the new team, three men brought in by Pinko were settling in, they also were Peruvians. It was clear from the onset that they did not want him around. He thought he would have a talk with Pinko, the company was paying him, but he wasn't doing much. He was fortunate to catch him; he was hardly in these days.

"We want you to be available all the time, Sidney." Pinko sounded anxious. "I appreciate your main assignment is now complete, but there will be many teething problems, I am sure, and Jose feels the knowledge you have of the war machine would be invaluable. We were also thinking that you could design and organise an exhibition using your model, maybe in a small temporary reception building, the portable type. What do you think? If you could we would be grateful."

Sidney was relieved, he was feeling a bit aimless, the murders had disorientated him and taken up most of his time. He found things confusing and couldn't see a clear path ahead. It was a relief when Frank rang. "We need to talk Sidney," his voice had an edge to it. "Things are not good, three deaths and one attempted is causing my superiors to question my working methods."

Sidney couldn't imagine Frank having superiors. "Do you want me to come to London, I do have time."

"Yes please, that would be a great help, Bob could bring you in his car, he could then give you an idea of the problems we are facing on the way. That would make our meeting easier; I would rather we keep Penelope out of this for the moment, you will understand why later." Sidney was feeling more positive now that he was being proactive, but at the same time apprehensive, it was the level of violence.

They set off next morning just after nine, less traffic. Bob was obviously briefed to talk. "The first thing we need is patience, all of us, your knowledge of the war machine is crucial to our plans. Frank has had further developments and he will discuss this with you, but only you would know how Goth Enactments could have created a deception, and we know they have." The traffic was sparse, and Sidney had time to think. It was a relief to know that there was a deception, he felt at times alone in his conviction of it.

"We understand your frustration Sidney; from the beginning you were convinced there was something wrong.

The point is: we now believe that the murders were a deliberate attempt by Goth Enactments to take attention away from the war machine, so that the true purpose of its manufacture would remain concealed."

"True purpose, what do you mean by that?" Sidney was desperately trying to understand.

Bob spoke in a measured way, it emphasised the seriousness of his statement. "It means, the war machine is going to be used as the description states, a true weapon of war. It will not be a plaything Sidney, an enactment, but the real thing. This is a twenty first century warfare machine in medieval guise."

"All this under my nose all the time, this gets more confusing by the day." Sidney's voice sounded bemused.

Bob continued. "The murders, instead of being a distraction, drawing attention away from the war machine has had the opposite effect, it has revealed to us another plan. Further facts have been revealed, Frank will tell you about that, my job this morning is to brief you on what we intend to do and see how comfortable you are with it. It is all a matter of trust, we feel that you have demonstrated that you are trustworthy, but you will need to sign papers if you want to be part of what we are proposing, it's just protocol.

His voice was calm and relaxed as he drove, Sidney felt nervous. "We are going to take action; the time is right for a pre-emptive strike. Goth Enactments have over-complicated things for themselves, too confident in my opinion, a flaw in the criminal mindset. We must avoid further deaths, you will be asked formally if you would like to be involved, you don't have to, but it would be helpful if you did, might save lives? Frank will explain." The rest of the journey was small talk.

It was the same office building Penelope and he went to on their first visit. But this time it was the conference room, which was situated on the penthouse level, it covered the whole of the fifth floor. A self-contained office area, the views over the courtyard were typical London. It was opulent, but not over the top. There was a tray on the long table, he could smell the freshly made coffee.

Sidney sat facing the courtyard, there was a huge central plane tree, it gave him a sense of normality, in this crazy situation. So, this was the secret world of government control, it all seemed a bit too plush and comfortable for that. These men were real though, and if a tough Inspector Buck accepted their credentials, so did he.

"Good to see you Sidney, I trust Bob's given you the low-down on the way up. And the general direction we are going with this. We would like you on board, part of the team, if you are willing." He handed Sidney a cup. "Coffee or tea." His voice was neutral.

"Coffee please," said Sidney, feeling he was acting a part in some film and all this was just fiction.

"Now, to explain if I may before you agree." He loosened his expensive jacket, the air conditioning was not working as it should, Sidney thought. "We had intended to arrest Pinko, Jose, and two committee members, Gwendoline Grace and Norman Keep, the ones you entertained." He smiled. "But your actions have meant a change of plan, Gwendoline has attempted to escape to Africa, she was arrested at London Airport, thanks to you she panicked, we had a tail on her." He pulled out a sheet of paper from his file.

"Miss Grace made a statement, she said that it had been arranged that Norman would follow her once the dust had settled. We have ensured that Mr Keep thinks she has gone to Africa and not in custody. "Frank sat back sipping his coffee: Sidney could see he was pleased. There was a prolonged silence, nobody spoke, Sidney then realised that perhaps they were waiting for him to respond to Franks proposition. He felt they were using the fact of Gwendoline confessing to entice him to join the team, a mutual challenge, he spoke out.

"Your suggestion, Frank, about me being part of your team, it would be a privilege, happy to help. Goth Enactments still want to use me, so I can be a mole in the camp."

Frank looked relieved. "We are pleased to have you on board Sidney, I know Bob wants to work with you; in these past few weeks we have all got to know each other, a good induction for a lasting relationship. And oh yes, we have a job for Penelope, in fact it's a job for both of you." Bob had a huge grin on his face.

CHAPTER 41
GRACE

"Gwendoline Grace is in custody." It was Frank, he asked her if she would go with Sidney to interview her, he had cleared it with her boss, Nick. She felt excited, some positive action at last. Frank said the team had done a thorough job, but if two people she knew saw her she may reveal further information to a couple of friendly faces. She was being held in London headquarters, the situation was becoming increasingly sensitive, any information you can get no matter how trivial it may appear could be helpful.

They went by train and tube and arrived at West Central police station at ten a.m. as arranged. They were taken to her cell, it was not a welcoming place, with its muted cold, grey colours. Gwendoline was sitting on a long hard bench; her face was expressionless, and her athletic body slumped. She recognised them, but her emotions did not register, her effort to keep control was evident.

Penelope wanted to feel sorry for her, but the woman was complicit in first degree murder. But her job was to get close, she was just about to launch into a charm offensive, when Sidney spoke. "Gosh Gwendoline, we were sorry to hear of your sad predicament, when we heard we thought a visit would cheer you up, they told us not to bring anything, not even cakes." He grinned cheerily. "Is there anybody you want us to contact for you—people we know perhaps?"

Penelope was impressed, if his disarming manner didn't work nothing would. Gwendoline's face crumpled, and she started to sob. There were no chairs, so Penelope sat next to her and put her arm around her shoulders. "This is such a mess." Her voice broken. "I didn't kill anyone, I told them, it was Norman—that man is a monster he's ruined my life." Her voice was getting stronger as the anger took hold. "He convinced me that it was all part of the war machine games, an enactment, I went along with him and I did help him, God forgive me. I didn't know the deaths were real, I thought it was all acting, he was with me all the time and wanted me around, I can see now that he got a kick from that. I told the police I didn't see much and what I did see I thought were actors. I am sure they don't believe me."

Her body shuddered in despair and she started to sob again. Penelope felt sure she was telling the truth. "We will try and help you Gwendoline," she said, "Did you know if Norman had anything to do with Jasper Thorndyke's death?" She composed herself and looked up.

"I have thought about that, I realised that was real, but I didn't know anything about it until afterwards. But I have since remembered something; I think the police should be told.

Norman has a collection of medieval weapons, they are not at his home, he keeps them with all his archery equipment, including mine. We both have a locker, they are large and can hold lots, the key for mine is in my car." With a consolatory hug from Penelope and a word of encouragement from Sidney, they left her to her misery. They had a welcome coffee before getting on the twelve fifteen to the City of Cry and its wayward residents, including Norman Keep.

CHAPTER 42
THE LOCKER

Frank was delighted with the archery club locker find. "We need to get access, best at night, I will arrange this through Inspector Buck, he will know who can be trusted, he may even attend the club." He grinned; they all knew Buck was antisocial. "However, there is always a risk that Norman Keep may be informed by someone, but we will make it known and in no uncertain terms, that if there is a leak, a price will be paid, Buck knows this.

Sidney was pleased when Bob suggested they take Penelope with them to the archery club. "It is less threatening to have an attractive girl on the case." His grin said it all. "Also, three heads are better than one."

The archery club was two miles from the city centre, it was a two storey, sad looking timber clad building of some age. The secretary, a Tony Townsend, was a cheerful type and accommodating. "I have the master key here." He pushed the key into the locker keyhole and turned it.

"Bingo." His voice was triumphant; it was clear he was nervous, the call from Buck had obviously rattled him. He opened the door and stepped back subserviently. The locker door was just over two metres tall and wide. Inside there were numerous shelves, these were packed with swords, axes, sabres knives and clubs, they all varied in size and shape. Most, formidable and gruesome in appearance, the sight was mesmerising.

They stood there in silence. Bob spoke first, "Mr Townsend, does the club have a licence to store armoury like this?" He waited.

"Oh dear no," he mumbled sheepishly, realising the lockers should be checked. "This is dreadful; what do you think I should do?"

Bob then took authority. "This is locked at all times, right! So, there is no danger to the public, which is our immediate concern and why we are here. So, we will not confiscate them today, we will leave them in your care." He looked at the man with a granite like stare. This is a police matter and all we want you to do is inform us if the locker is used or anything is removed. We will fit a camera by morning to cover the locker door, all movements will be recorded, so don't be concerned just monitor and inform. A plain clothes officer will be around we will give you his mobile number."

Before they left the three of them photographed the weapons without disturbing them, there were some unidentifiable. Sidney thought they might be implements of torture, and that cheered them up no end. "I know a chap we can consult," said Bob. "I will email him the images and get back to you both."

Sidney was beginning to feel the evil in the man. Norman Keep must not be underestimated, he maybe planning another murder. Where and how was one thing, but the why remained a collection of unrelated facts.

CHAPTER 43
RIGHTS

Herbie would be mortified if he knew that another tunnel had been found, connecting the under-croft to Battle-Cry Castle. This would mean Historic England could have precedence and take control of public access. Herbie wouldn't find out until a full inspection and survey had taken place, or if he looked carefully himself. He was sulking now, so unapproachable. Herbie loved to be in control, but he wasn't. Sidney knew it was his own fault, he never listens.

He would admit that he did miss the verbal clashes with Herbie, he was a knowledgeable man, though not practical and prone to fits of panic for no real reason. But he would have a real reason to panic now. He had purchased a house at a high price, which left him in debt and the crowning glory, or the subterranean mine, would be removed because of Historic England's rights.

Sidney pondered over a way of engaging with him again, a sulk is a tough nut to crack. The answer came from an unexpected source, Herbie himself. He was acknowledged to be an expert in medieval weaponry. Herbie's reticence to communicate lately had left him out of the loop. So, what better person to consult him about the hoard, someone who could smooth his prickly spines—Penelope.

"My feeling is, I think I had better see him alone. I am sure he wants to be in on what we are doing, but we must go to him, it's a male pride you know." She grinned at Sidney. "His pride will be really dented when he finds out about the second tunnel, Sidney muttered.

Herbie wanted to meet her at his office. "I have lots of books there, we can talk about what I have found out from the images you sent me. They were interesting and I have some matches."

His office was close to the castle and was the upper part of an old stable block. "Hello my dear." He welcomed her in with an old-fashioned bow, she felt slightly embarrassed.

"This is Sidney's computer; he usually works here." She guessed that might be a hint that he wanted him back. "I have all my books on medieval weaponry here." He patted a pile of large, expensive looking books. "I have put markers in each one of interest. And more importantly, for each of the types of weapons used in the murders." He opened the computer and brought up the first image of the opened locker. "Now, you can see here." He pointed on the screen with a pencil. "This is a medieval mace, and here another, just the two, there may be more, but I couldn't see. The first murder was committed with one of these I believe, could be from this collection. A forensic examination may connect the murder weapon to this collection, just a thought."

He opened another book. "Now, this is the type of crossbow that could have been used in the second murder, and the bolt. He enlarged the computer image. "Here are some of the bolts in Norman Keep's locker, look closely and you can see scores in the shaft, these can be distinctive and peculiar to the weapon and the chances are that if it was one of these bolts that killed Billy Bowman, you have your man."

He scrolled the computer again. "Now we come to Rose

Archer, a musket ball was her demise—so I believe." He said it in a tone that assumed a fact, but Penelope guessed he had inside information. "The measurements should be checked against these and the method of foundry casting; could have a cast iron case here." A faint smile flickered across his face; he was not normally one for jokes. "Finally, Jack Spear; there are several spears here in the photo and it is not possible for me to make comment until I have inspected the weapons. And the murder weapon of course, but I can say, to throw a spear, or javelin, for any distance requires considerable strength and skill."

Penelope thanked him for expertise and the typed report on his findings and agreed to scan and email these to Sidney. There was now a strong case building up to assume that Norman Keep was the perpetrator of the murders.

CHAPTER 44
GOTH

Chief Exec Diego Jose had requested a meeting with Cry City Council. His request was formal, and he had sent with it an agenda for the meeting. This outlined his concerns about the recent events and the lack of progress in resolving matters for the war machine to be up and running. More importantly, he wanted to discuss the legal implications of the newly discovered vaulted under-croft. There must be accountability when a legal framework is in place, he had sent the agenda to all those requested to attend. This was political warfare, thought Sidney.

Sidney was looking forward to it, he felt that Goth Enactments may at last remove the veil of secrecy surrounding their activities, but what would be revealed? It was going to be interesting and he was disappointed that Frank would not be able to attend. Sidney was there as an employee and he requested that Bob attend as security consultant, he was surprised they agreed to that, Frank was pleased.

Attending for Cry City Council: Penelope Pride was there as a planner for Nick Tweed, Head of the Planning Department and Nick would act as chairman and host, there was no legal representation there for either side.

Attending for Goth Enactments: Herbert Strange, consultant, Sidney Picket, Bob Bloom, both employed by Goth Enactments. Diego Jose Chief Exec and Pinko the company's engineer as the applicants. Bob Bloom as a government agent would be the ears, he had a recorder.

The reality was the only ones loyal to Goth Enactments were Jose and Pinko, the other five attendees were their adversaries. A fact that they were blissfully unaware of. Jose was intoxicated with power and Pinko following in his wake. Being drunk with power dulls the senses, particularly common sense. And the meeting was opened with a sense of foreboding.

Nick Tweed was a master harmoniser and tried his best to pour oil on troubled waters, but his best was not good enough. Chief Exec Jose transpired to be a force to be reckoned with. "You have all read my statement I sent you—I hope." He glared around; his tone had revealed a steely impatience.

Sidney felt uncomfortable, he wasn't the one being questioned, which was a relief. He had found the man formidable at the first meeting, but this was at another level, he had achieved what he wanted and was now fighting to keep it. His next words had menacing undertones.

"My request for clarification on why my planning permission cannot be fully implemented is clear; please respond." He looked around the table, a contemptuous look on his face.

For a few moments nobody spoke; Nick Tweed took up the challenge. "Thank you, Mr Jose, I would like, if I may, to remind everyone that there have been three murders and an attempted murder, on or near the war machine." He paused to let the power of the words sink in. "These tragic deaths have had, I am sure, a negative impact on your project, but also the discovery of the medieval under-croft. With respect, Mr Jose, I do not think anyone is at fault here, it is just extenuating circumstances caused by criminal activities."

As Nick finished, he emphasised the last two words and stared intently at Jose. The man was undaunted. "I tell you what criminal activity is, not allowing my ramp to be built as my legal planning permission states—that's criminal." His face was red, and his eyes glittered out of the deep folds in skin.

Sidney thought highly of Nick and would try and support him without compromising his own position as Jose's employee. It was Penelope who took up the cudgels on behalf of the council, her voice measured and calm. "You are aware Mr Jose, I am sure, that the weight of the war machine has considerably increased and is now seventy tons over the designed weight, which was forty-five tons. So, the ramp structure sitting on the ground needs to take a moving war machine with a total weight of one hundred- and fifteen-tons gross, that is, unless you have more weight to add?"

She stopped for a moment and put the master plan on the table. Jose was too angry to respond quick enough, Penelope swiftly continued. "We have taken technical advice and the ground geo-survey did not go deep enough to reveal the under-croft. Therefore, this council cannot be responsible for your own specialist's lack of due diligence.

Sidney was impressed, Jose wasn't and looked lived, Nick was suppressing a smile. It was Pinko, the engineer, who deemed it appropriate to take the topic further.

"Miss Pride—gentlemen, it has always been the vision of Goth Enactments to enhance and enrich the cultural and historic values of the City of Cry. We did suggest that we could cut the ramp short when the vaulting was discovered, but we did not receive a favourable response, so you can see why we are frustrated." It was a good bit of diplomacy, thought Sidney, but the impact of Mr Jose's previous scathing attack and financial threats could not be brushed under the carpet.

Then Chief Executive Jose pitched in to add weight. "You are being too kind Pinko; let me make it crystal clear gentleman, and a—hum Miss Pride. I am insisting on the ramp being installed as per the planning permission. That will be put underway immediately, you can take whatever legal steps you have to take, but it will incur costs." He sat back; arms folded.

Sidney felt the time was right to support his boss, but he would need to choose his words carefully; Jose's plan of action was ill conceived. "May I say at this point, that having been involved from the beginning under the expert eye of Herbert." He glanced at him and smiled. "I feel we are in danger of losing sight of the original vision, as presented to the committee, and just as importantly, the outside entertainments manager of Cry City Council." He paused to let his statement sink in. "It is the vision that Mr Jose is concerned about."

He hadn't said much, but hopefully his loyalty to Goth Enactments would be acknowledged by Jose. Herbie spoke up. "Actually, it was the entertainments manager who told me, that because of the gruesome murders there are countless coachloads of tourists booked up solid, to come and see the scene of the murders and experience real medieval war conditions on the war machine. It has become worldwide news. Come and see The Crime Scene of The War Machine, is the media chant." He looked around; Sidney guessed it was for applause.

Sidney then looked closely at Jose; his face showed no sign of emotion. A thought had occurred to Sidney, were the murders designed to cause public interest and increase footfall. This would mean, in effect, that Jose was the murderer, albeit by proxy. He brushed the thought aside.

Herbie's statement had changed the tone of the meeting and in fact terminated it. Sidney reckoned Jose thought that things were getting too close for comfort. There was no conclusion, and a killer was still at large, he would need to keep close to Jose, if he were to get to the truth.

CHAPTER 45
REPORT

Bob had made his report out for Frank, he had prepared his own notes of the meeting and he had recorded it as well, he sent a copy to Penelope and Sidney. His conclusions were disturbing, but not surprising, thought Sidney. All the evidence pointed to Goth Enactments as being the perpetrators of the murders, that is Pinko or Alberto Pedroso his real name, and Chief Exec Jose.

Sidney was at a loss, why should they take such huge risks. The waters were well and truly muddied now and the situation did not lend itself to a long-term solution. So, he met Penelope to talk it through.

"I come back to the thoughts I had some weeks ago," she said, "That the changes in the design of the war machine may mean it is being prepared for some evil purpose. Oh, and yes, what about the accommodation inside, that's weird. We have slowly got used to the situation, but all I can say is, what's it for?"

Sidney agreed with her. "Yes, it's strange how everyone accepts the unusual because the war machine is unusual, and I might add so is the applicant." He stopped, grinned and looked at Bob's notes again. "Yes, it's here," his voice excited. "It has been staring us in the face, the gist of it is this. Bob is saying that—Mr Jose is a manipulator and a bully. His attitude at the meeting was not as a full-time investor, but as an asset stripper.

The other point Bob makes, which is more revealing, it is the tenuous investment platform created by the manufacture of the war machine and at an enormous cost. There is not tangible value here, so there must be another agenda, maybe for another use. And he feels, it can be assumed it will not be for lawful entertainment."

Sidney looked out of the window and absentmindedly stirred his coffee. "It's all so confusing," said Penelope. "I have been keeping some notes, part of my job—perhaps we can go through these sometime.

Sidney could see she was trying to be helpful. "It's the technology in the sling arm that bugs me," he said, "I had a thought a while ago that because this was such a sophisticated installation, it might be a high-tech device for radar or such like, but how it would be used I have no idea. And like Bob, I feel sure it is nothing to do with tournaments."

"Gosh," said Penelope. "That will set the cat among the pigeons, what convinced you both?"

He pulled out a notebook from his bag. "For me it is the costs: as we were building the war machine, I prepared a programme and that included the initial costs. After that Pinko said not to bother, he would be dealing with the finances and for me to make sure the work was being done, on time and to spec."

He put his notepad on the table. "I would say, with the amount of money they have injected into the venture, the interest alone will be staggering, that is if its borrowed. Also, the gate fee, or cash generated by the war machine will not be enough to cover it. And now Jose wants to go head and build the rest of the ramp over the vaults—more costs."

The coffee house was getting crowded, news of the war

machine murders had attracted public attention and at mid-morning the High Street was buzzing. They decided to go for a walk, along the High Street and over the bridge, taking a stroll along the riverbank. "I couldn't think with all those people about; maybe we will get a better perspective of the situation from this side." Hand in hand they made their way downriver.

"I must be honest with you Penelope; these delays are making matters worse. The war machine should have been in action by now," his voice expressing frustration. "It all seems a bit of a lost cause now; it is getting too complicated for me; I hope Frank and Bob know what they are doing."

He felt her hand squeeze his arm. "There are a lot of people involved now Sidney, you are not alone; we must rely on the professionals.

CHAPTER 46
THE ENEMY

Sidney had put the suggestion to Frank and Bob, that they should use Penelope to communicate with Norman Keep. Penelope and himself would meet with him on the war machine to discuss the way the shields are being used, ask him for advice on the way they would protect the war machine from fiery arrows. It was for authenticity when filming. "That is the ploy,". said Sidney. "There will be lots of people around, Penelope, so we will be safe, the police have also sealed off the church spire from access—it's a crime scene."

She looked enthusiastic he thought, but he was not sure it was a façade for his benefit. He decided he would discuss openly with Norman Keep the current security arrangements and how archery would fit in to advantage. He had to admit, it was a vague plan, but Bob would also be invited as a security specialist. Bob was familiar with the criminal mind and could hopefully judge the man's reaction to various questions.

The main question would be, how did Norman feel about the shields fixed on the exterior of the war machine and was this authentic. He hadn't been consulted before because the team had no idea of his experience in archery. Penelope phoned Norman, who said he would get back to her, he did two hours later, Sidney suspected that he had consulted Jose or Pinko.

Sidney felt a sense of unease, meeting a suspected

murderer on a nice sunny day seemed bizarre. Penelope was bright and chirpy, and Bob came dressed in his security uniform. Norman Keep came in an outfit that could only be described as the ultimate in military surplus specials. His leather flying jacket, the prominent item of apparel. It was obviously important to him to portray a masculine presence, particularly as he had been invited by the delightful Penelope Pride.

Norman had arrived a little late and they watched him walk towards them in a slightly rolling gait, reminiscent of a fighter pilot in an old movie. They greeted him with friendly handshakes. Sidney realised then, when seeing him away from the formal atmosphere of the committee room, that there was something off key about him. His cultivated manner of dress of course was one thing, but there was something else. It was the continuous, barely concealed smirk on his face, as though he knew a secret that he wasn't going to share. Sidney shivered, he felt it was the expression of a murderer suppressing an eager desire to tell of his gruesome deeds. His cold demeanour, when revisiting the scene of his crime was telling.

Bob took the lead, much to Sidney's relief. "What we were discussing Norman, was not so much the medieval pageantry of war, but the nitty gritty of it. A lot of it will be filmed in detail, and as a specialist and local, you would be the ideal person to advise, at a fee of course, Goth Enactments are keen to get it right." It wasn't the suggestion of money that opened Norman Keep up, it was his ego. Sidney reckoned that the thought of him doing his master Jose's bidding, but at the behest of the victim and being paid, was too tempting an opportunity to miss.

The meeting after that went smoothly, Norman's graphic descriptions of a medieval war and gore, left Sidney in no doubt that they were dealing with a seriously warped character. The only extra facts gleaned out of the meeting, was a better understanding of the power of Goth Enactments. Also, Norman did let slip that he did know Pinko on a personal and social level. That clinched it for Sidney; the man was in their payroll and a dangerous enemy.

Penelope looked relieved when the meeting was over. "I think we will be having problems with him; he is unpredictable. And will he murder again? Frank and Bob should bear that in mind. I think it was right to see him though, he was left unsuspecting, I hope."

CHAPTER 47
THE SCIENTIST

Alan Berry the scientist turned up again, Frank had emailed Sidney and asked him if he and Penelope would meet at Cry railway station for that morning. It was dull, drizzling and damp. They met him from the train at nine fifteen a.m. Frank had said it was important to meet him, he had interesting information for them.

"Hello Penelope, Sidney." Alan thrust out his hand enthusiastically. "I would have worn my medieval chainmail, but it would get rusty in this weather." He grinned, then grimaced as he looked up at the darkened sky. "I suggest we find a private place to talk. I need to show you some information I have collected."

Because of the weather, Sidney had brought his car. "To be assured of a quiet place to talk, I thought we could go to the local Travel Lodge Hotel, is that OK Alan?"

He sat happily in the back of the car. "That will be fine by me."

It took fifteen minutes to get there and parking was easy. Sidney ordered them coffee and they settled themselves into three large, sumptuous leather chairs. Alan sat opposite them, the etched glass topped coffee table between, it was certainly quiet.

Alan perched himself on the edge of his chair and laid out some drawings and plans on the table. "Just to let you both know, I have explained my theory to Frank and Bob, and they suggested I meet with you both, because you know the war machine as well as anyone." He picked up one of the drawings on one of the sheets. "This is a detailed drawing of a typical satellite communications tower. Now I don't expect you to fully understand the detail straight away, so I will explain. In simple terms each communication tower, and there are many dotted around the country, send microwaves in a vertical beam, straight up into the air to contact a satellite or satellites that orbit the Earth."

He spread out another sheet, it was an aircraft flight chart. "I have four of these here, they cover all the flight paths that are located over Cry City and heading towards London. You can see here, clearly, the location of the satellite communication towers and the flight paths avoiding them. My theory is simple, and I am surprised that no one has thought of it before. You can see the towers or masts are no-go areas, aircraft are instructed not to go near them; the vertical beam of microwaves from each tower can have catastrophic effects on the navigational and electrical systems and can cause failure in the planes ability to stay in the air."

He stopped for a moment allowing the information to sink in, he then continued, but more earnestly this time. "The risk is minimal if the aircraft passes over at speed, but still a risk, but," He looked at them both, his face eager to convey his discovery, "if this technology was housed in the war machine slinging arm, and I think it is, we have a controlled beam that can follow the flight path—can you see where I am going with this—that is why the alignment of the war machine was such a crucial part of the planning permission documents. Sidney, you have just built a war machine that can silently shoot planes out of the sky and no one would ever know." He paused, looking intently at them. "In one day, the annihilation could be a minimum of fifty planes dropping from the sky over London, that's fifteen thousand souls, not counting those on the ground, a massive loss of life. With radio silence, no one will understand what is happening, nothing can stop it, this will change the worlds perception of warfare.”

Penelope and Sidney were mesmerised and horrified by these startling facts. Things were starting to make sense to Sidney now, particularly his disjointed relationship with Pinko. “I have to say at this point, Alan, that since the new team for working the war machine have arrived and taken over the final fitout, I have been locked out. I can see now why.”

Alan sat back in his chair for the first time and gave the appearance of relaxing, he stirred his cup slowly deliberately waiting for a response. but his words had made Sidney’s heart start to race. It was Penelope who spoke first. “This is frightening,” gasped Penelope. “We must do something— what can we do?”

Alan had a focused look on his face; his answer was not straight forward. “Frank would normally swoop, close the whole thing down and order a full investigation, but it’s the three murders and one attempted that causes him concern, he is desperate not to incur further deaths. His view is, all the time we conduct a non-threatening stance, we can keep the status quo and avoid the risk of the killer striking again. Frank feels it best to gather more information first, before Jose and co make a move and use the war machine in earnest—there should be time.”

“So, we carry on as normal,” said Penelope. “Don’t you think it’s dangerous? and what about Norman Keep, he’s a loose cannon, or should I say bolt.” Her attempts at light hearted banter failed. The conversation was now drifting into the what ifs and maybes.

Alan soon showed signs of wanting to depart; he had fulfilled his mission; the field work would be left to the likes of Frank and Bob.

CHAPTER 48

Detective Inspector Buck was disgruntled, he had a feeling that things were afoot, but he did not know what. He felt sure it was the London mob, Frank and Bob were a thorn in the flesh. On top of that his chief was putting the pressure on for results and the media were doing the same. Pride would not allow him to ask Frank and Bob, so he asked Sidney Picket to come to the station. Most people summoned to a police station would normally be nervous, he would push Sidney for information, intimidate him with his authority—yes that's it, be sure to get a result that way.

Sidney was surprised at the call and intrigued, he wondered what Buck wanted. He arrived at the station at ten fifteen a.m. as requested and waited twenty minutes before being led to a room on the first floor. Detective Inspector Buck was waiting, with a burly policeman in uniform. "Take a seat will you," he said abruptly, it was a command, not a request. "I have a file here." He looked down at the opened file. "It describes your involvement with Goth Enactments." Sidney said nothing, he sat passive making no movement or acknowledgement, it was not a question.

He continued. "It states that you designed the war machine, is that correct?" His voice demanding.

Sidney answered promptly, "Yes, that is correct." Buck knew this, so why ask? He sensed that the man was on a fishing trip for information he couldn't get elsewhere. Sidney knew

Bob didn't rate him highly, so he thought he would play games. "You know Bob Bloom of course, well he informed me that the only reason Goth Enactments had been given approval to the war machine was because of a generous donation to the Cry City slush fund." Bob had gleaned this from the early morning street cleaner when on evening shift, so it might or might not be true, but interesting, nevertheless.

"Slush fund?" Bucks voice expressed concern, which wasn't surprising it must have smacked of illegality. "Are you saying the rules have been broken?" He sounded eager for facts.

"That's the word on the street," said Sidney, literally he thought and continued. "I haven't got proof, but my feeling is there is truth in it." He hoped he wouldn't be pressed further, bringing Bob into the dialogue would maybe deter him.

He decided on another question to distract him. "We had a meeting with a Norman Keep, a planning committee member, we asked him to pay a visit to the war machine. He has considerable knowledge of war techniques and is an experienced archer; he will be helping us on the practical details. Oh, and by the way, have you any news on Billy Bowman's death?"

The meeting wasn't going to plan, Sidney was asking too many questions. "We will keep you informed, Sidney, on any developments regarding the murders, as may be necessary. In the meantime, could I ask you to keep me up-dated on any new developments, I don't want any gaps in my file.

CHAPTER 49
FIFTH

The fifth incident happened in a manner that surprised the police but shocked the nation; it was televised. That fateful evening in June would be etched in Penelope's mind, so vivid was the experience it would haunt her dreams. It was six forty-five p.m. on a Saturday, and the seething mass of humanity in the City of Cry showed no sign of abating. The annual festival was in its second day and the atmosphere electric.

Sidney had joined her, and they walked arm in arm amidst the colourful, noisy, excited crowds. This year was different; the council's entertainments manager had arranged for a hot air balloon to be inflated and suspended at three hundred feet over the castle grounds. The public could then have a bird's eye view of Cry City at a fee—there was a long queue.

The war machine was not yet commissioned, the grand launch was to be mid-August, so it became a static attraction that caused great interest. Then, the general hum of the festival was broken by piercing screams. Sidney looked around, then the screaming started again, but this time near him, he turned, people were looking up and pointing. It was the balloon, it appeared to be slowly falling sideways, and there were arrows sticking out of it. And two more hit as they watched, followed by more screaming.

They were mesmerised, not knowing what to do, feeling helpless as the scene unfolded, or as the balloon imploded.

Slowly, gracefully the balloon started to collapse and sink to the ground. Three hundred feet quickly became two, then one, then at fifty feet a miracle happened. A gust of wind, aided by the, now overheated hot air unit, slowed the rapid descent down to a soft drifting fall and the basket gently touched the green turf.

There was a sound of spontaneous cheering and clapping as the occupants of the balloon's basket shakily got out, but safe. They could have been killed and possibly the public beneath. The televised coverage went viral, the City of Cry was worldwide news again. But this time, for what was an attempted mass murder event, covered by the media in glorious colour and sound.

There was one beneficiary however of this disastrous happening, the people who advertised their company on the side of the balloon. In bold two-metre-high letters the statement was clear. AVOID THE ARROWS OF MISFORTUNE: Invest in our RISING company, for a profitably future.

The balloon had been in place for the past few days, plenty of time for the archer to think of an obvious solution to bring down this huge, hovering target, helped of course by the advertising. Sidney was trying to analyse the person's tactics, the first question was, where did the archer fire from and he had an idea about that, and then who? His first thought was Norman Keep. He needed to talk to Frank.

Frank was looking at the coverage live, he phoned Sidney. "Yes, Frank I am with Penelope, we watched the whole thing. The arrows appeared to come from the direction of the castle, but unsure, difficult to say with the balloon moving about and changing direction. I will try and get the arrows, but I expect the police will be all over the scene, I reckon they may have come from Norman Keep's collection.

Frank and Bob were at Battle-Cry Castle at eight p.m., it was a two-hour drive. DI Buck was waiting for them and Buck's men had collected all the bolts that had been fired, there were fifteen in all—a crossbow had been used. They had been fired into one small area of the balloon's fabric for immediate and maximum effect; the pressure of the hot air did the rest.

Sidney was standing with Penelope within the cordoned off area of the crime scene, but at a distance from the basket, which sat on the ground looking forlorn with its deflated balloon spread out on the grass. The police had taken over the castle grounds and the public were kept at a distance. The noise of the festival was still going on, though subdued. Buck wanted to talk police matters with Frank and Bob; Penelope and himself were not included. The man has control problems, thought Sidney; he turned to Penelope.

"It could have been so much worse," he said, "The fact that there were no fatalities is nothing short of a miracle. The situation is getting out of hand, no one is safe anymore and Frank must be annoyed, he wanted to avoid this sort of thing happening. He is probably kicking himself that he didn't arrest Norman Keep at the time—waiting for evidence is a bit risky, it seems to me."

Frank and Bob soon left Buck to his organising and came over. "Pleased to see you both." Sidney said and proceeded to relay what Penelope and himself had witnessed, he then voiced his opinion. "I didn't want to interrupt your discussions with Buck but having thought about it I think it would be prudent to check the roof of the north tower of the castle keep, the one with the flagpole." He pointed to the corner facing and nearest the balloon basket. "That is over one hundred feet from the ground and the ideal place to fire up at the balloon, which I think was anchored three hundred feet from the ground."

"OK," said Frank. "We will get Buck's men to check it out, but I doubt whether the archer would leave any clues." Bob nodded at that and walked away dialling on his phone. "I have also asked Buck if the cache of weapons at the archery club have been touched and he said not." He frowned. "But I am not happy, do you have those images you took of the locker still on your phone Sidney?"

Sidney produced his phone and scrolled up the shots he took. "Here they are." He handed the phone over.

Frank looked carefully at the images. "Yes, I remember now, the bolts for the crossbow are in bundles, look on the shelf, there are several, must be sixty or seventy bolts altogether. We need to get to the archery club now, is that possible?"

"We can go there now," said Sidney. "The club may be socialising, but if not, we will get Buck to organise an entry."

It took ten minutes to get to Sidney's the car and twenty to get to the club. It was open, and Mr Townsend was available. Sidney took the initiative; he had met the man before. "Sorry we didn't ring you before coming, Mr Townsend, but we urgently need to check Norman Keep's locker again, is that OK?"

Townsend looked blank for a few moments. "Oh, didn't you know, all Mr Keep's equipment has been removed by the police; they came yesterday afternoon."

Sidney was shocked, they all were Buck had told Frank they had not been touched, perhaps he didn't think they would check. Frank had been specific with his instructions, leave the weapons there. Frank nodded again to Bob. "Buck," was all he said, Bob turned and was immediately on his mobile.

That man Buck is an idiot," his voice icy calm. "Or something else." He showed Mr Townsend his credentials. Norman Keep's locker was empty, he then insisted that all the lockers in the club be opened, this took over half an hour. They left the club leaving Mr Townsend looking perplexed. Penelope was sitting in the front with Sidney driving.

"I am not sure I trust that man," said Penelope. "He would be loyal to the members first, before anything else."

"I agree." Frank's voice was almost a snarl, he then spoke to Bob in a similar manner. "Bob, were you able to arrange anything with our Mr Buck? I need to speak with that man urgently, and his chief. Sidney felt uncomfortable and sorry for Buck, to be confronted by a formidable force like Frank would be an experience not to be forgotten. He was relieved to be driving.

CHAPTER 50
SUSPICION

Penelope was slowly getting used to being part of the team, but found it challenging. Nick, her boss had been informed by Frank that her services were needed. To help the police with their enquiries, was the official statement. At least she could concentrate on the matters in hand and forget the workload, which no doubt would be growing daily, it was the department's problem not hers. Comforted by her own assessment of the situation, she met Sidney for breakfast.

They sat in Don's, amidst the smell of mouth-watering toast. "I think Frank is taking over now," said Sidney. "DI Buck has fallen from grace big time, and Frank outranks him, and his chief." Penelope tried to concentrate, but secretly wished the whole business would come to an end. She wanted an ordinary relationship with Sidney, not one where she felt like a gangster's piece of fluff.

"Are you OK?" his voice showed concern.

"Yes—yes of course, just getting into the swing of being associated with the police. Feel a bit like a spy, that's how it seems." She smiled, softening the harshness of her statement.

"OK," he sounded relieved. "Bob tells me Norman Keep has disappeared, but he is emailing Gwendoline Grace, Frank of course is controlling her replies. Apparently, Norman wants to join her, he thinks she's in South Africa, he would be caught if he tries to leave the UK."

She knew Sidney was enjoying the action and did not want to put a damper on his enthusiasm, but it had to be said.

"Sidney, I need to explain something, he reacted to the tone of her voice and looked pensive. "Working at the council offices, I hear things in the cafeteria, lots of gossip mainly, but also information which can be credible and, in this case, too much of a coincidence. I was told yesterday, by asking innocent questions, that DI Buck is also a member of the archery club." She felt guilty that she hadn't phoned him, but she had been so busy. "Sorry should have phoned you."

"What!" Sidney was incredulous. "Why didn't he tell us, or rather Frank or Bob. You know what this means, Penelope; we have a detective inspector of the police force using the same locker room as the murderer, his position is now compromised, we must tell Frank and Bob immediately."

Penelope looked at Sidney and replied. "Oh dear, we must have looked through DI Buck's locker after the balloon drama, it was rushed; we should have checked the names as we went along."

Sidney phoned Frank and put his mobile on loud-speak. "OK, Sidney, I understand. Buck is completely out of order; I will have him stand down immediately. In the meantime, we need to find out where Norman Keep's weapons are. If they are not at the station, heads will fall, I can promise you that."

Penelope was once again reminded of the seriousness of her position and felt sure that Frank had a higher status than that which he portrayed. His voice over the phone then took on a softer tone. "I have instructed Bob to be available, at a moment's notice, at all times. Both of you are at risk now, I don't want another drama like the last one. If Buck is suspect, others may be as well. But don't worry all will be well, will speak later."

They walked from Don's towards the river; Penelope still wished it would all end.

CHAPTER 51
CRY HOTEL

Frank had booked into The Cry Bridge Hotel; things were moving too fast to waste time on travel and Bob was nearly a resident anyway.

Penelope and Sidney arrived at the hotel at nine thirty a.m. as requested. The ground floor reception room was quiet, and Frank and Bob were waiting, the pleasantries were skipped, Frank quickly launched into his plan of action. "I still believe that Norman Keep is being used as a distraction, so assuming that is the case, what are we being distracted from?" He looked around, though not expecting a response. "I believe it is connected to the war machine. With Norman Keep causing total mayhem, Jose and Pinko are creeping along unnoticed and the true nature of the war machine goes unquestioned."

Sidney could see how Pinko had played him, it was annoying that the man wasn't being challenged and now Buck. "How will you be dealing with DI Buck? I thought he would be a key player?"

Bob responded. "We have put DI Buck into custody, he is refusing to talk now, but the weight of evidence is so telling against him, it is only a question of time and he will crack. He is not a strong character."

"Again," said Frank. "Buck is a distraction; we must put our brain power to better use. Let go back to the beginning; what is the war machine designed to do? Please don't say it's for throwing water filled balloons." He grinned and waited.

"It's the power and electronics that intrigues me," said Sidney. "When Alan, the scientist, popped down to see us, he seemed convinced it would be used for aiming destructive micro-waves at commercial planes flying overhead, is that a credible theory? And how can we prove or disprove it?"

Frank leaned forward and in lowered tones said. "We mustn't close in too fast on Pinko and co, we need hard evidence. Bob has reasonable access to the war machine, but not all areas. It could be ready for use now, for all we know, but it's a risk we must take. If we strike too soon the consequences could be disastrous, we must be sure of our facts.

Sidney's head was buzzing, he could see the wisdom in that, but the action of Norman Keep, the balloon saga and the three murders, what about them? Surely caution must be thrown to the wind, but he kept quiet and waited. It was Bob who came up with a practical suggestion.

"The war machine arm must work off a power supply, we know there are generators, but Pinko admitted that these are just back-up, and the main power will be from the national grid, but why is such a lot of power needed? I thought it was intended that the war machine will be pulled along by hordes of people using ropes."

Sidney felt prompted to make a comment. "Well, Bob, we could get the electricity board to cut them off but knowing Pinko they would have a backup plan."

Franks mobile rang, he answered, he listened for a few moments; they waited. "Buck has cracked," he said, but his voice sounded sceptical. "But he has come up with a story that doesn't make sense, it involves Herbert Strange."

Sidney became nervous, but not for himself, he knew how impulsive Herbie could be sometimes, to impress, rather than use his common sense. He waited to hear the bad news. "DI Buck claims he was acting on information given to him by Herbert Strange," said Frank. "That, by removing the cache of weapons, valuable evidence would be preserved. I think he is telling stories, but best follow it through."

Sidney thought he would redirect the discussion away from Herbie. "Alan Berry, the scientist; can I say that I found him to be a very astute man, not one to be lost in fantasy, so, in all seriousness I feel we should be looking at his theory with an open mind; for myself, I believe it is in fact the truth and it is what is happening now, under our noses." It was the first time he had pushed his views forcibly in front of professionals; he waited.

Frank looked stern. "I have to say Sidney, you have voiced our own fears, I agree with you, but we must not lose sight of the fact that there is a murderer intent on causing harm in the here and now; fact not theory."

Penelope had been silent, obviously waiting. "I have been giving some thought to the legal aspect," she said, "my boss, Nick, is sympathetic, but tries to avoid conflict, he has instructed me to do the same. Now of course, I can view the situation from a different perspective, and I have concluded that the only way we can impede progress of the war machine is to use the planning permission." She put a document on the table. "The key is the condition put on the approval by Historic England on the construction of the siege ramp. It specifically addresses their concerns regarding the weight distributed over the area of ground it sits upon. It is a historic site and under the ground there is a strong possibility of ancient artefacts being present. The level of loading now proposed will cause untold damage, as the newly discovered vaulting has highlighted." She paused to allow her findings to sink in and concluded, "I am therefore recommending we challenge Goth Enactments to stop work on site, as from immediate effect."

Sidney was surprised at her forceful approach; Frank responded. "There is only one flaw in your recommendation Penelope; Goth Enactments will immediately be alerted to our resistance to their plans."

Penelope did not want to give up easily. "We could inform Historic England that the planning permission is not being adhered to and work should stop until the matter is sorted out; it will give us time. They have a vested interest in the vaulting underneath that area of the site."

Frank smiled. "Well Penelope, I think you have hit on a solution there, but with Jasper gone, will it be difficult to motivate them?"

She smiled back, obviously pleased at his reaction. "Nick will back me on this one, HE respects him, and I am sure he will arrange it."

Frank suggested they meet up on a regular basis at the hotel to discuss strategy, in the meanwhile Penelope was to deal with Nick and Historic England.

CHAPTER 52
MR STRANGE

Herbie phoned Penelope first, he suggested that the three of them meet up as a matter of urgency. She thought it unusual for him to ring her, Sidney would have been a more appropriate, but she had sensed there might be some friction between them, bearing in mind Herbie's secrecy concerning the existence of the hidden medieval vaults.

He wanted to meet them at the archery club of all places; bearing in mind what DI Buck had been saying about Herbie, it would be difficult for them to go with an open mind.

Herbie was there with Mr Townsend, of the two, Herbie cut the finest figure, if only by his size. He wore a vintage hacking jacket with his usual cravat, Penelope thought he had a sheepish look about him, maybe it was the gossip. "Thank you both for coming." His voice measured, "I have asked Mr Townsend to join us for a moment or two, he would like to explain himself, it might be useful."

He looked at Townsend, who cleared his throat. "Yes— well of course." He coughed nervously. "It's like this; Mr Herbert Strange is our technical adviser on the maintenance and manufacture of the medieval long bow and arrows and the skill needed to use them." He cleared his throat again, he looked uncomfortable.

"We are mortified here at the club, to hear of the three tragic deaths and a near miss." His emphasis on the last word suggested that it couldn't be one of the members, they never miss. "As a reputable archery club, we do not condone such wanton acts of violence." He stopped, obviously struggling with his emotions;

Herbie stepped in. "Quite—quite Mr Townsend, murder in any form is abhorrent to us all, and to associate this with the club is, quite frankly lamentable. Thank you, Mr Townsend you have made your point, —thank you." Mr Townsend made a rapid exit.

Penelope was relieved, she found him a little on the furtive side, she felt sure he was hiding something, they waited for Herbie to speak. He looked uncomfortable, but did his best to appear relaxed, it didn't really work. "As Mr Townsend said, I am a member of the club, but only active in the sense that I advise on the procurement of arrows and equipment, I do not fire them." Penelope felt uneasy, it was his nervous manner. "Now you may know this, but a long-standing member of our club is DI Buck, a policeman, I think he is investigating the murders." He looked about to see that they were not in earshot. "There was talk among the members that he and Norman Keep were up to no good, I don't know how true it is, but not smoke without fire—I say."

Penelope looked at Sidney, he nodded. "Can I say something in confidence Herbert," she said.

He nodded. "Please do."

"Sidney and I were informed that DI Buck had accused you of advising him to remove Norman Keep's equipment and weapons from here and take them to the station. I have to ask, is that true?"

Herbie's jaw dropped, and his eyebrows shot up. "What— he said that, what utter nonsense, the man's a liar, I did no such thing—why should I?"

Penelope could see he was genuinely upset. "Sorry Herbert, but we needed to ask, we know the police will ask you, but we thought it better from us."

Herbie's face was red. "My God the man's a rogue of the first order and make no mistake, if you can't trust the police, who can you trust?"

Penelope felt sorry for him, he was going to be devastated when he finds out about the second tunnel and Historic England's ownership. His flimsy castle he had built on hope, was going to collapse like a pack of cards.

CHAPTER 53
RADAR

It was Bob who discovered it, but only because the new operational crew of the war machine had been sloppy. They had left a radar antenna in position overnight and had hastily concealed it first thing in the morning, but not before Bob had seen it. Why have a radar antenna? It was no use for manoeuvring a medieval war machine, it was looking like Alan the scientist could be right.

At first light he took a few shots on his mobile and emailed them on to Frank, who in turn asked Alan the scientist what he thought. His response was, I told you so, they are tracking planes passing overhead at night. Sidney wondered what Frank would make of it and would he act. He was surprised at Frank's reaction, he called for an urgent meeting at the hotel.

His opening words were harshly spoken. "We have a problem. We have discovered a connection between the Peruvian company Goth Enactments and Russia, we believe it is KGB, it is a tenuous connection, but real nevertheless and sufficient to send alarm bells ringing in Whitehall." Sidney was amazed, the situation was getting more bizarre by the day. Frank continued. "As you know, for Bob and I, national security is paramount and our main focus."

He looked at Bob and nodded. "In my nightly duty," said Bob, "I have found signs that some, if not all of the operational crew are Russian speaking. I speak Russian myself; part of my SAS training and I have no doubt of it. That is one aspect, but the other is the Peruvians, they have been sloppy in their handling of money. We have traced the source to Russia via Switzerland." Bob stopped and looked around grinning with satisfaction. "We have also discovered that Norman Keep visited Moscow four times in the past eighteen months." There was long silence.

"Surely DI Buck can't be a spy as well?" Sidney looked at Penelope, was she thinking that he was? Herbie, Townsend, Buck, Norman Keep, and the common denominator: archery. Three deaths and a near catastrophe all by the power of the bow. He decided not to say anything, it could be just a coincidence, but Herbie did find a lot of money to buy Castle Ditch House. He hated himself for thinking such thoughts, but it was the direction the facts were taking him.

CHAPTER 54
FACTIONS

Sidney's suspicions were aroused again. The house sparrows had flown their nests and the ensuing morning silence allowed his doubts to grow, as he lay looking up at the ceiling, pondering over the day ahead. Frank would be expecting action from him, but Pinko was also expecting a day's work overseeing, it was what he was paid for. He didn't see that Frank would be offering expenses, but now, he assumed, he must be in the employ of HM Government, in some way or another.

The action that Frank wanted, was for Historic England to call a halt to the work on the war machine. Sidney found it confusing, but it didn't seem to bother Frank, he was obviously used to dealing with the criminal mind.

He dressed slowly; it was a dull day; he decided to wear a suit, he could think sharply and logically in a smart suit. The growing suspicions had taken shape and form in is mind. There were two factions he could identify. Firstly: Goth Enactments and their secret weapon and secondly: Norman Keep and DI Buck with death and destruction following in their wake. Sidney sometimes found logic hard to follow, human beings had a habit of being illogical.

It was clear from the start that Pinko and Jose had distanced themselves from the local politics, and even the war machine operatives were an enigma. Certainly, it was not possible to connect Norman Keep's activities to Goth Enactments. Penelope was right; stop Pinko and Jose in their tracks, this will then provoke them into action, probably in retaliation, which hopefully will reveal their true colours. It was a little bit of hope value, but he wasn't trained like Bob and Frank in the machinations of criminology. His experience was limited to the sometimes-illogical planning decisions made by the logically minded committee.

They sat in Don's coffee house. "I have been told that Jose shall be receiving the court order later this week," said Penelope. "It is to stop work on site immediately, we will see what they will do then. My feeling is they could have become a self-contained self-sustaining unit anyway, and able to carry on, on the pretence that they are looking after the site, I suppose that would include you Sidney.

He immediately became concerned. "How can we monitor what happens when they are tucked away in the war machine? I think they may be in their rights to be there."

Penelope made a sympathetic comment. "I think we should consider that we are, in effect, a couple of amateurs at this type of business, so don't be too hard on yourself. I am sure we will find a way now that Bob and Frank are leading things."

He was annoyed with himself for appearing to be a bit out of his depth, it was more the cloak and dagger stuff that got to him.

"Let's walk over to the church and have a look around, we may find a bit of inspiration." She wanted to break the tension.

The vicar was out, but the verger was helpful, he recognised them both and was eager to talk. "The reverend is on holiday for two weeks," he said, "but I am pleased you popped in. In view of the recent events, I think you need to see something important, it's in the crypt, have you got time?"

"Of course," replied Sidney.

They followed him down a narrow, circular stone staircase and at the bottom was a large gothic shaped, old oak door. He opened it and they walked into the vaulted church crypt. It appeared to be the same size as the nave above. "It's along here." The lighting system was good, and the area was clear, apart from a little storage put near the door. They followed the verger to the far end, and he approached a large door with rusty hinges, he produced a key. "This is what I wanted you to see." He unlocked and opened the door, the door opened towards them and they stepped back. Facing them was a tunnel running back into the darkness. The verger switched on the lighting, revealing the tunnel to be about ten metres long.

"This tunnel runs to the west, directly towards the vaulted under-croft that I believe you have discovered. I am aware it's been a bit hush-hush and the vicar said that we mustn't get involved and there are probably old plans of it anyway."

They approached the end of the tunnel and facing them was a stone arched doorway bricked up. "This is amazing." exclaimed Sidney. "This is the third tunnel entrance to the under-croft, Historic England will be pleased, not so sure about Herbie though."

They thanked the verger for showing them the tunnel. He said he would inform the church commissioners, when the vicar got back from his sabbatical holiday. As they walked away Penelope was exuberant. "What an amazing coincidence, I am sure the vicar wouldn't have been so accommodating; more the spiritual type I expect."

CHAPTER 55
CUSTOMS

Frank and Bob seemed so relaxed and professional; it did not occur to Sidney that they would be armed. They met in the Battle-Cry Hotel as usual. They listened with interest to Penelope and Sidney's account of their new tunnel discovery, but they soon focussed their attention on the matter they wanted to address. "Norman Keep is back." Franks voice was harsh. He thinks he is meeting Gwendoline Grace at London Airport tomorrow, we got her to text him to say she was returning to England, it's all been arranged; he doesn't know it's a trap."

It was then that Sidney saw Frank's gun, he glimpsed it as he relaxed and allowed his jacket to fall open. It was well concealed. He wondered if Penelope had noticed it. "You know Mr Keep reasonably well Sidney; I have a marksman covering the passenger terminal that Mr Keep will use to pick up Gwendoline and another four plain clothes men standing by. We have pictures of him, but we want you to pick him out for us before he gets to Gwendoline." He looked intently at Sidney.

"I will arrange a headset for you, I also suggest you wear a baseball cap, or a woolly hat." He laughed, Sidney had never seen him laugh before, it wasn't unpleasant. Frank looked at Penelope. "You will be quite safe Sidney, but I don't want you to get anywhere near him, leave it all to us."

The plane was due to arrive at eleven forty-five p.m. Frank insisted they all go together in his car but have a backup police car to escort them there. Penelope was to stay with Frank and Sidney with a plain clothes officer from Frank's department. Bob would be leading the armed squad of four, there would be no outward signs of officialdom and they would be mingling with the public.

Sidney, normally immaculately dressed, turned up wearing a colourful, tasteless outfit, seemingly tailored for an exotic destination. His cap and dark sunglasses completed the image of an inexperienced tourist that was so noticeable, he became unnoticed, but not in the car going up, Penelope giggled.

Sidney became alert, his shadow, one of Frank's meanest looking agents, nudged him gently in the ribs. He looked in the direction the agent was looking, and there no mistaking him, it was Norman Keep in the throng of waiting people. "Yes, that's him." Sidney felt nervous now, he hoped Norman wouldn't recognise him. He was about twelve metres away from Keep, who, it appeared, was concentrating on the arriving passengers filing through the customs check.

Gwendoline Grace appeared a little way back in the queue, she had a small shoulder bag, which she then removed to carry and place on the short conveyor. She looked up briefly, furtively, Sidney thought and then occupied herself with following her bag on its brief journey. Sidney looked over at Norman Keep; he had seen her as well and was pressing forward eagerly. There was no advantage in this, there were too many people, but his anxious face said it all, he was totally focused on her and oblivious to all around him. Love is blind and he was blind to the fact that Bob and three armed men were closing in.

Sidney thought that Norman had taken a risk, but then he wasn't Norman Keep. The reasoning of a murderer, bloated with success from killing and elated with a feeling of invincibility, cannot be understood by a normal person.

The speed and efficiency of Norman Keep's capture and disarming, he had a small handgun, warranted a medal. That was the view Sidney expressed later, though it must be said his view was influenced by the fact that he knew what was going to happen and relieved when it did.

Norman Keep now joined DC Buck, bringing the number of captured miscreants to two. "I have a feeling this isn't the end of it," commented Frank. "In my experience hardened criminals are harder to catch; even though one is a policeman, they are not of that calibre."

CHAPTER 56
H.E.

Debriefing, is probably the word used for it, thought Penelope and the ensuing, excited discussions following Norman Keep's capture, certainly gave that impression, albeit in a hotel reception. "The point I wish to make here," said Frank, "is this, how much, if anything, do Jose and Pinko know about our activities. We are closing in now and I don't want them alerted, one of my men was instructed to focus on getting hold of Keep's mobile, he did, and I am waiting for a report back on its contents. Do any of you have any comments?"

"I do have a point to make," said Penelope. "And that is; we must assume that Norman Keep and DI Buck kept in touch with Jose or Pinko on a regular basis, in which case, they, that is Jose and Pinko, will be wondering why this has stopped. I think we should be pressing Keep and Buck to try and find out if that's the case."

"Thank you." Frank smiled. "We have this in hand; DI Buck is in a mess, his career is ruined, and his position is now hopeless. I think we can get what we want from him at this point in time. Our Mr Norman Keep however, is not what one might call ordinary. He is a triple murderer and bent on causing mayhem, but how someone like that could be involved with Goth Enactments, I am unsure." Penelope noticed his gun again; he was obviously relaxed about letting them know he was armed.

He continued. "We have a specialist interrogation team on the case now, led by DI Janet Jones, there are four of them in the team. They will take it in turns to interrogate, four hours each session, he will have a lawyer present of course, but their technique is sharp and relentless and guaranteed to wear him down. Each one of the interrogators is a specialist in a particular field of human behaviour, I don't envy Mr Keep, if he has a weakness, they will find it."

Frank replenished their coffees. "Now to our own tasks. Sidney and Bob have key positions relating to the war machine and will be able to give us a clear picture of Jose and Pinko's activities and possibly an idea of their future plan of action." He paused. "I know it will be difficult, but you guys must maintain an air of normality at all times; we must not alert them. I will team up with Penelope for the next few days, there are issues I would like to discuss with her about Cry Council and Historic England. I think we should meet tomorrow morning and go through the documents and drawings I have obtained."

Penelope could see the wisdom in this the course of action and working with Frank would give her a better overview, though she would miss Sidney; she responded. "You recall meeting my boss, Nick Tweed, head of planning the other day, well I feel it would be a good idea for myself and Frank to meet up with him on a confidential basis. I feel sure he has information that would help us. He would be more receptive to outside pressure—I am too close to him."

CHAPTER 57
BANKS

Historic England had appointed another case officer to take over Jasper's position, his tragic death had caused a major reshuffle. Because of the recent important historic underground discoveries at Battle-Cry Castle, it was deemed necessary to have someone of a certain calibre, they chose Miss Mary Banks.

Mary had a reputation for possessiveness, a quality much needed in conservation. She took on the mantle of a mother hen, and her brooding knew no bounds. She wanted to meet Penelope and peck away at the files; her first aim was to see if Jasper had missed anything in his Historic Statement supporting the planning application. Tactically, it was important for her to find fault. She could use misdemeanours in many ways and there were bound to be some, even spelling mistakes, to build a foundation for taking control, which was the only way to satisfy her possessive nature.

Penelope was nervous, Mary's reputation had gone before her and they had never met before. Her misgivings however were ill-founded, mainly because Mary saw a planning officer as a kindred spirit, a natural comrade in the war against nasty developers. They hit it off straight away, Mary was like herself in many ways, same age, attractive, assertive and a rebel with a cause. She agreed immediately that the action taken, to put an injunction on the works was the right thing to do, she obviously liked a fight.

They met at Cry City Council offices; Penelope had all the files available and a meeting room had been booked. "I must say you are having a bit of a battle, Penelope; I don't envy you, but I am here to help so let's see what can be done." The first file that she opened for Mary was relating to the planning condition concerning the weight of the war machine, she passed it to her.

"Thank you," Mary said. "I have been looking at this condition and I feel we need to be—a bit more assertive." This was her favourite saying. "I think a meeting with highways would be of benefit; the ground taking the ramp that the war machine is running on, should come under the classification of a road. Now this throws up many complications and it is complications we need if we are to stop the works permanently. From my point of view, and I will express this formally, the idea of using historic ground for this incredibly heavy war machine to run up and down is ridiculous; would you be allowed to build a motorway here? I think not."

Penelope was encouraged, she had been feeling out of her depth lately and meeting Mary Banks had brought back her confidence. She was sure Sidney would be pleased to know that they now had an ally and one with a strong—no nonsense personality. He needed support, they both did and having Mary part of their team could only do good, she would pick a moment when she would suggest it.

Frank asked if, Bob, Sidney and Penelope would show Mary the under-croft and tunnels. "She needs to get the full picture from you three; reports miss out a lot of the detail."

Penelope got the keys from Herbie, she thought they should come clean about the extra two tunnels they had found—but after their visit. It would be better coming from Historic England, she felt sure Mary Banks was used to public announcements. Herbie would be upset, but that couldn't be helped, it was nobody's fault.

They met at Castle Ditch House at nine a.m. Sidney worked from seven a.m. at the war machine which was a five-minute walk away. Penelope introduced Mary to Sidney, she had already told her she and Sidney were an item. Bob introduced himself. Mary blushed as she shook hands with Bob, Penelope was surprised, her normal tough exterior had melted away. "Shall I lead the way," said Sidney and promptly walked over to the basement stairs, they followed. Herbie's temporary lighting was the same, adequate—just.

The visit was a success on two levels; the first, the highest level, was the chemistry of love taking place between Mary and Bob. It was charming to witness but had an impact on the way matters were discussed by the high level of giggling and inane banter between the two of them. Penelope exchanged amused glances with Sidney.

The lower level of success was the information that Mary had on the buried Saxon king. The police tape over the vault area was still in place, but all inscriptions were easily discernible.

After looking around as best they could in the dimmed light, they congregated in the centre of the under-croft which was at the extremity of the light penetration. Mary had stopped her girlish chattering and the four stood in silence looking around and into the darkness. "I must say, there is something strange about this place." Mary spoke in hushed tones. "You will notice the vaulted arches towards the castle side are different to those on the wall facing the church." She pointed to at the tall Norman arches on the castle side. "These are very ancient, and I suspect are part of an earlier structure. Jasper pointed this out in his, sadly incomplete report."

She moved towards the castle side. "What he didn't report was the existence of Roman remains—here—here and here." She pointed excitedly. "This vaulted area we are standing in has all the hall marks of the under-croft or subterranean area of a Roman amphitheatre. What a find, we are the first to recognise it and therefore discover it." She walked over to Bob and put her arm in his, he grinned.

"Amazing." Penelope felt excited and part of a special occasion. "I know I have mentioned this before," said Penelope, "but we need to get all of this under-croft surveyed, it can't still be a crime scene surely?"

Bob walked towards the centre again. "Strictly speaking it is," said Bob. "But a survey could be carried out with a policeman in attendance to protect the scene. You know of course that I am a policeman, just thought I would mention it." He smiled at Mary, she blushed again.

The rest of the day was spent pleasantly enough, though Mary and Bob's growing relationship was difficult to cope with at times. Oddly the seriousness of the political situation they found themselves in, only seemed to add fuel to Mary's incessant giggling. Penelope didn't remember love affecting her like that, or at least hadn't been aware of it, but then had she fallen in love yet?

CHAPTER 58
BANKS

The dynamic between the two couples was the bond of lasting friendship, if love lasts. Their next port of call was to show Mary the war machine. "We thought it best if you saw the under-croft first," said Sidney. "This will give you a better picture of the impact the heavy structure will have, I am aware you know already, but when you see inside you will fully appreciate the magnitude of the problem." The four of them made their way over towards Sidney's office where Pinko would be waiting.

Pinko looked slightly edgy but put on a pleased to see you look; he never came in before ten and had the coffee on. "I would like you to meet the young lady from Historic England I spoke about, Miss Mary Banks," said Sidney. "Mary, this is Pinko my boss, and engineer in charge of the war machine."

They shook hands. "Nice to meet you Miss Banks, I hope you find the workmanship up to your expectations." To say the following exchange was frosty would be harsh, but the injunction was in place and Pinko must be feeling the pressure, she would be regarded as the enemy. "May I suggest we make a tour of the site first," he said. "The logistics of building the ramp will be of interest I am sure." His tone was controlled and neutral.

Mary's professional status was being highlighted by the power she wielded, it was obvious the injunction would be talked about and she was not one to avoid conflict, quite the reverse. They followed Pinko out and along to the contentious part of the ramp closest to the castle wall. There was no ramp from the battlements, a thirty-metre section was missing because Goth Enactments were not allowed to build that section. Another contentious issue to be addressed by Mary. Jasper had been a bit too arrogant in his approach to the problem and Pinko's reaction was understandable.

"May I suggest we walk along the ramp towards the war machine." The four trotted after Pinko. The ramp was over ten metres wide and constructed of massive chunks of hewn oak laid across the width. The war machine was back about forty metres from the end, and the iron railway style tracks needed to be avoided, there were awkward gaps. "This might be difficult to walk on," said Pinko. "But when the war machine is pulled by manpower, the hundred or so men pulling it will need a firm foothold." They cautiously walked towards the enormous medieval structure.

They completed their stumbling walk along the ramp and finished at the foot of the war machine. It towered above them, the multi-coloured shades of glittering shields, gold, silver, white, red and green, shining in the sun hanging on its sides like a cloak on a giant creature.

"Gosh," exclaimed Mary. "It's so big when you get up close like this; it's a bit like a windmill. I must say I do like it; pity about all the teething problems." Her words were meant to encourage, but the word 'big' tempered the compliment with a note of criticism. Pinko, turned without comment and led the way to the rear entrance door. They followed him in. Sidney was dumfounded at the transformation; no expense was spared he thought. It was state of the art office accommodation. Bob's idea of clearing it out seemed nonsense now when looking at it.

Sidney felt uncomfortable, Pinko was being too polite. He was usually like this when on the defensive, which was not surprising, given the level of investment. He wondered how he was going to react to Mary. They were inside the reception area in the War Machine now and the atmosphere was tense, due to all of them being so close to each other.

Now Mary had an otherworldly way of speaking when confronted with owners of period properties, it detached her from the devastating news she might sometimes need to bring. Like, bringing the news to some proud period property owners that their precious roof timbers were not from the *Golden Hind*, this needed that special detachment that she had carefully cultivated. This was so convincing, that the owners usually felt sorrier for her, than they did for themselves.

In this instance, given the high-profile nature of the project, Sidney guessed that Mary would need to have done her homework, he wasn't to be disappointed. Pinko showed signs of nervousness; he had two attractive, but aggressively professional young ladies to contend with and two fit, dynamic young men looking on. He tried to take the lead.

"Goth Enactments is a high-risk commercial venture, which is now in danger of failure, due to a legal notice having been served to cease work." Pinko looked at Mary and then at Penelope. "Sidney has done a first-class job and I am sure he would agree with me when I say that it is crucial, that we carry on and finish the works."

Sidney nodded sympathetically, and Bob decided to say something, if only to justify him being there. "I have been talking with Sidney about this and I have a suggestion to make.

As you know I am on night security and consequently able to see things in a different light." He grinned at his own pun. "It seems to me, that there is more furniture and general office storage and clutter than is necessary to work the war machine. If all this were to be removed it would reduce the weight of the war machine by two, maybe three tons easily." Pinko showed no emotion at this statement. To Sidney this was a warning sign, they couldn't afford for Bob to lose his position, he decided to defuse the growing tension.

"Bob is trying to help here; personally, this is the first time I have been inside the war machine for nearly two months now and it takes some getting used to."

Pinko ignored him and turned to Mary. "Now Mary, may I call you Mary?" Pinko's voice had a slightly ingratiating tone, which didn't suit him. "As a company we pride ourselves in doing a good job; this awful saga started the moment the under-croft was discovered, none of this is our fault; all I am trying to do is avoid things getting worse." It sounded plausible, but Sidney could see his words were like water off a duck's back to Mary.

"I would like to put things in perspective for you Mr Pinko." Mary emphasised the Mr, knowing Pinko was not his real name. "You were given planning permission by a committee on the basis that you would execute the works as presented to them at the formal planning meeting. At that meeting a scaled model was produced and formed part of the permission information. Now Mr Pinko, I put it to you that if you inspect the model of the war machine there is no internal accommodation shown there, the model is over there in the corner."

Pinko half-heartedly followed them as they gathered

around the model in its glass case in the corner of the reception area. Mary began her next attack, turning the already fraught meeting, into a battle zone—it was now war. This was the skill she had cultivated and the reason she had been chosen. She moved in for the next verbal attack.

"Your name Mr Pinko, appears as the applicant on the planning forms, and planning permission was given to you. But this is not a real person, Mr Pinko does not exist. You have used a fictious name, what is your real name, could you tell us what it is please?" Mary's question was simply put, but the tone demanded an answer, Pinko said nothing, she continued. "If the planning documents are seen to be falsified, I am afraid it brings into question the validity of the permission. This is now a legal matter and must run its course, therefore no further work can be carried out without a ruling from the courts. I am sorry to inform you of these findings."

But Sidney could tell she wasn't sorry. Pinko, white faced and shaking with anger stormed out and left them alone in the war machine. It was the ideal time to have a good look around, Pinko had requested the operation team to make themselves scarce for the meeting.

"We know the war machine is bugged," said Sidney. "So, no swearing please, it may offend."

CHAPTER 59
REVELATION

The next morning meeting at the Battle-Cry Hotel included Miss Mary Banks, which was no surprise to Penelope and Sidney. Frank seemed to take it in his stride, but by the faint smile on his face he knew love was in the air. Another face that turned up was Alan Berry the scientist, but he was singularly lacking in his usual medieval banter, and his jaw was set in a determined fashion.

Penelope found this odd and unsettling; Frank ever sensitive to those who worked under him, decided to deal with Alan first. "You mentioned on the phone, Alan, that you had something to share with us." His voice was soft and friendly.

"Well—yes I have," he replied, tentatively, his eyes glancing around at the group. "I am afraid I have some disturbing news for you." He stopped and fumbled with his coffee cup. "Actually, it's disturbing and exceedingly exciting at the same time." His following remark was intended to take away the doom of the first. He opened his holdall and produced a folder, and out of it he pulled several plans and spread them on the coffee table.

"I have spent some time at the local archives, in fact a lot of time and copied these old maps I found; one goes back to 1320. Having studied these in detail, I have come up with some information that may explain why this company, Goth Enactments, are acting the way they are. Some of it is fact, but

I have based my theory on calculated assumptions, the first being the real motivation and reward—money and I think that is a fair calculated assumption." They were mesmerised, they were seeing a different Alan, this was Alan Berry the dedicated researcher and scientist with a bit between his teeth. His normal shy and reserved manner hidden behind jokes, had gone.

"Now, look here." He pointed to an area on a map showing a long strip, lightly shaded red. "I have shaded this to show the position of the siege ramp, as constructed and in position. You will see that the ramp follows the line of an original early structure which formed part of the castle fortification. It is difficult, though not impossible, to do a ground penetrating survey with the ramp there, but I am sure Goth Enactments would have done one and are aware of what's beneath the ramp and that's why they built it there in the first place." He paused for a moment and seemed more relaxed now that he had discharged his revelation.

"I see now," said Sidney. "That's why they only wanted me to be involved in the war machine and not the ramp, the ramp was well underway when I arrived on the scene. It is puzzling that's for sure, what do you think they have been doing?"

Alan produced another drawing, this time it was a section through the ramp and showed an underground void. "Now we come to my assumption, I am sticking my neck out here, though my conclusion is logical. For reasons yet to be revealed, I think Goth Enactments had gained access to the underground structure, or vaulting, at the time the ramp was being constructed, satisfied that what was there suited their purpose, they then continued with the building of the war machine, which, as part of the project is only a cover."

Sidney looked at the plan. "This fits with the initial difficulties I had, communication with Pinko was virtually impossible."

Frank had listened to Alan's explanation and Sidney's response and said, "The bit that confuses me is the work they have done on the sling arm, such a lot of sophisticated design carried out and to what end?"

Mary spoke out. "I can tell you now, from looking at the 1320 map, that they have discovered something special and are trying to hide it. They have the advantage of a digital survey, but I think we can overcome that by doing one ourselves, ramp or no ramp." She grinned. "Historic England have the authority and that is who I work for, so let me know when and I can put it in hand."

Penelope was excited, their team was growing stronger and she felt more confident that things would work out. Though there was still a lot to understand, particularly about the murders, how on earth did they fit into the plan? Her optimism and naive confidence would be short lived.

CHAPTER 60
THE SURVEY

The first event was shocking and unexpected, DI Buck had committed suicide, but how he had achieved that was a mystery. "That needed inside help, or he's been bumped off," said Frank; he was furious. "I wanted to interrogate him myself, we need to check on Norman Keep, we don't want him going the same way. If anyone wants me, I shall be at Cry Station."

Sidney left them at the hotel; it was midweek and now this, his head was in a whirl; he was busy, and now it was getting complicated. He had arranged to see Alan later. Alan Berry had organised a geophysical survey for the strip of ground the ramp was built on. The company he had instructed had signed a confidentiality agreement and agreed to work at night, between the hours of midnight and four in the morning, and this also needed to be flexible. It was government department contract, so they would be discreet.

It was obvious now that Pinko regarded Bob as a risk, he had been too outspoken at the meeting with Nick Tweed. "I have arranged for you to have company in the evenings, Sidney," he said, "I think having two security men is now more appropriate, he starts this Monday evening." There was no question of discussing it. That gave Alan's men two clear nights to do the survey, he hoped that was enough time to cover the whole of the ramp. It was and it was completed in two; the results were sent through to Alan, who took great pleasure in forwarding a copy to the team.

"There is a tunnel," he said in his email, "that runs under the full length of the ramp, it is five metres wide and is six metres from the ground level to the bottom of it; it averages four metres in height. You will see from the drawing that the walls are a metre thick and it is cross arched and there appears to be various sized objects scattered along its length, large and small."

For Sidney, this was a tantalising glimpse into an ancient mystery, it was old and certainly abandoned long ago, but what was it used for? He sat studying the email and the scans, he had stuck copies on the wall of his flat and he was relating these to the whole site, including the castle.

Looking at the plan there were now four new tunnels found, including the one Alan had just revealed and all leading into, or from, the newly discovered amphitheatre or under-croft structure. Was this where the combatants entered to fight. He was hot with excitement at the thought of it, he wondered what Penelope and the rest would make of it.

Sidney's excitement was dampened by Bob's call. "Hello Sidney, sorry to bother you, but it's about Herbert Strange, Frank has been doing some homework and it would appear that Mr Strange purchased Castle Ditch House with borrowed money and this seems to have been arranged by Goth Enactments. There is a connection between the two parties, without a doubt, I must go, speak later."

Sidney thanked him and was disappointed that there was no mention of Alan's discovery, he was just left with another piece of the jigsaw to be put in place, it was sad, but from now on Herbie could not be trusted.

Mary phoned and said she would like to meet up, just the

four of them, it was important. Sidney wasn't surprised, Alan's discovery was ground-breaking, in more ways than one. They met up late afternoon on Monday, Bob would be starting his first night shift with company.

"The reason I wanted to meet up like this was so that we could have open and relaxed discussions, before putting any ideas we have to Frank."

Sidney suspected that she was intimidated by Frank and her boldness was probably a protective stance, but he liked her and felt she could do a good job. They had met in Sidney's flat, he felt it would be less stressful there, more relaxing. "The more I think about this," said Mary, "the more I am convinced that we are on the cusp of a major archaeological breakthrough. And I also think Goth Enactments are aware of its existence and its significance, and that is the problem we must wrestle with. What are they doing, or what are they going to do with this discovery? they do not own the land only lease it at a peppercorn rent, they certainly don't own what's under, or in, the ground"

She was sitting next to Bob, who looked adoringly at her, obviously enchanted. Sidney hoped he had not lost his tough sharp, SAS trained mind in the euphoria of love. It was Penelope's following statement that left them dumbfounded. "What if Goth Enactments are the equivalent of tomb raiders, and they are going to take what they can get, this underground tunnel may contain treasure."

"That would be amazing, but it makes complete sense to me," said Bob.

"And me," said Sidney.

"Well, I must say I join all of you in that," Mary said grinning. "And to ask, what shall we do about it? Perhaps we should be doing the raiding ourselves."

CHAPTER 61

"We are forgetting the murders and now one suicide." It was Frank's way of gaining their attention. "If we are not careful, we shall miss the point and the point is, why was it necessary to kill three people and potentially more and why should a person involved kill himself?" He had their attention now. "If these murders are linked to the war machine tunnel, let us call it that, as there are now three other tunnels, it can mean only one thing. These dreadful acts of carnage are worthy of the gain and on that basis the prize must be enormous." Frank waited for a response from the four, they wanted to sip the tasty hotel coffee, but this was more important.

"How can we find out?" Mary though new on the scene was keen.

"Well Mary," replied Frank. "Money is usually the first motivation, then power and prestige, people have been known to murder for both; but I am convinced however, that these murders and all the shenanigans that went with them were intended as a distraction, no more than that. To keep prying eyes away from the real prize, the artefacts in the latest tunnel, I would use the term—treasure, but we mustn't get carried away."

He spread the geo-survey sheets out on the two coffee tables, he had shuffled along. "Have you noticed," said Bob, looking at Sidney. "The war machine has never moved an inch from the position it was built in, is there a reason for that? I thought it was mobile and ready to roll along the ramp."

Sidney was immediately alerted, Bob was right. "It is ready," he replied. "It can be moved along the full length of the ramp if necessary, if we had enough rope and many strong arms, but Pinko said it should stay where it was until the fuss of the weight problem had died down."

Mary was leaning over the survey scans. "I notice that the only section of the tunnel not surveyed," she said, "is under the war machine, if I wanted to get down into the tunnel from the top undetected, it would be through the floor of the war machine."

She looked around, Frank's face was beaming, obviously pleased she was part of the team thought Sidney. "Absolutely right, Mary, that is the first thing we need to do—we check it out."

He looked at Bob. "Ok Frank, it will be my first job tonight."

There was a new sense of purpose and comradery in the team now that they had a meaningful plan. After weeks of confusion and endless speculation morale had sunk low. This course of action was, in part, based on assumptions, but it was calculated and made sense; spirits were high, and they were expecting positive news from Bob.

Mary did not live locally and travelling every day to Cry City was time consuming. Penelope invited her to stay with her and her mother for a week or so, for her to be available should problems occur, she wondered how Frank would deal with her boss on this one. Given the complexity of the ever-changing situation, it was a sensible move. Mary promised not to discuss any matters connected with the war machine, or the tunnels, in front of her mother. But she could talk about Bob if Penelope could talk about Sidney.

CHAPTER 62
NIGHT SHIFT

Bob needed to be alone. His new security guard partner, a man called Luke was on time and eager, but fortunately inexperienced and poorly briefed. Bob took control in a natural, but firm friendly way and agreed a rota with him. "Best that we are equal in everything we do Luke," said Bob. "That way we avoid any misunderstanding and ill feeling." Because Bob was army trained and sounded like it, Luke automatically fell in line and went on his first tour of duty, he would start at the top of the war machine and work his way down, checking into every room and ticking off his list.

Bob reckoned he had at least half an hour free to explore the ground floor of the war machine. It took ten minutes to find it; there was a small cupboard on the main side wall. He found a trap door in the floor, it wasn't hidden and looked ordinary, the sort of access you would expect to find in a structure that was off the ground. For inspection maybe, perhaps that is what it is?

It had a ring pull, he lifted the hinged hatch and pulled it back. It was not just for inspection—that was for sure. His torch had revealed spiral metal steps dropping down into the darkness. His torch picked out the rubble and hewn stone surface of an ancient structure which must be the outside wall of the tunnel. They had dug a shaft down the side of the tunnel for the staircase, presumably to gain access in the side rather than through the top. From what Mary had been telling him, this was an illegal activity, without a permission.

The stair shaft was about two and a half metres square and his torch revealed the bottom as he crept down. The excavation, which was at least six metres deep, must have been a logistical problem. Getting rid of the material secretly would also have been a challenge.

He could just make out a rugged opening in the side wall of the tunnel, he had no time left to go down and enter, it would have to wait another opportunity, Luke must be getting near, he quickly took some pictures on his phone and made his way back up. He had shut the door to the cupboard behind him, so hardly likely Luke would try it, but best be prudent. He opened the door and stepped out into the reception area, no sign of Luke.

He was excited, the staircase was professionally constructed using scaffolding with stair components and a robust job. It was obviously designed for carrying materials up and down? He forwarded the shot he had taken to each of the others, it was now ten fifteen p.m. and so hopefully they would pick them up. His phone buzzed; it was Frank.

"Brilliant Bob, well done, I can see it's been constructed large enough to transport things up and out. I couldn't see properly; is there a door in the side of the tunnel?" He sounded excited. "No Frank, it's just a roughly formed opening; the wall is incredibly thick; I will look inside when I have more time." He spoke in whispers. "I haven't got much time now, I must go." He rang off, he could hear Luke coming down the main stair.

He waited for him. "All OK, Bob," he said, "It's very high at the top, I could see the city lights. There are some rooms that are locked, is that normal."

Bob suspected, by the tone of his voice, that he was expected to ask him questions, he responded innocently. "Oh yes that's quite normal, though I don't visit here often, I expect they have valuable computer equipment and such like stored away. Security, the way we are doing it right now is the proper way to do it, me on my own is risky; that's my view, but of course it's expensive labour wise." He hoped when Luke reported back to Pinko, any suspicions he had would fade.

CHAPTER 63
THE PLAN

They met up in the morning as usual, nine a.m. sharp. Bob and the others were buzzing with excitement from the evening's activities. Sidney for reasons he would rather not explain to the team, did not share in their excitement. The death of DI Buck he found disturbing, it was only four days ago, and Jose and Pinko were too close for comfort, and they did pay his salary. So, was it guilt? He didn't think so, fear more like. Just because something new had turned up, didn't mean that Norman Keep's actions should be forgotten, maybe another assassin would be sent in his place, what then?

He envied Bob's SAS experience; he had no training whatsoever himself, in armed combat or combat of any description, and here he was potentially in the middle of a war. Frank opened the meeting. "It is clear from Bob's delicate investigation last night, that Goth Enactments are up to no good. They are acting illegally; we are sure of that, but why take such risks? That is what we need to find out."

Sidney tried to concentrate on being positive, things were moving at a pace and he could feel danger, the others seemed oblivious to it. Any thoughts they may have had of the recent violence seemed to have vanished, or so it seemed. He would have to rely on Bob and Frank's combat experience, he was wondering if they had any, more doubts.

Frank wanted to demonstrate a proactive attitude, "I could

send in an armed squad and raid the place, but where will that get us. We could end up looking fools and lose the initiative. We don't know enough; we need to gain access to the tunnel first and end the speculation once and for all; it's facts we need." He looked around, his face determined; he had the authority to do what he liked, but a joint plan of action was always best.

Sidney was relieved, Frank was showing wisdom and if they could do what he had suggested it should end well, his thoughts were optimistic and based on hope. Bob gave his own optimistic take on it. "I have thought about this," he said, "and I think I could keep Luke occupied at the top of the war machine for perhaps an hour and a half. The rest of you can then go down into the tunnel and see what's there."

Frank brightened up at that. "Good idea Bob, can we do it tonight?"

"My feeling is," said Bob, "that Luke knows there is an access down to the tunnel entrance and he assumes I am unaware of it, so all the time I am not near to it, he is doing his job. So, the likelihood of you being disturbed is remote, but I would suggest you make it a quick visit and be careful."

Frank grinned in approval. "Ok Bob, you get off home and put your head down, we will organise torches and anything else we might need.

CHAPTER 64
THE TUNNEL

Bob arrived at five thirty p.m. one hour before his shift, he needed to be ready. Luke arrived and picked the keys up from Pinko. As they made their way to the war machine, Bob filled him in. "I would like us to work together this shift Luke, if that's OK, I thought I would leave you alone on your first shift last night so that you could get familiar with the place." He studied him for a reaction, he seemed relaxed. "That way I can give you some pointers on the way the company works and maybe you would want to make some suggestions as well, I am always open to new ideas."

He could see Luke was relieved; Bob wanted to come across as reasonable and someone just wanting to do his job. "I thought we should start at the top again, like you did yesterday and make our way down. You are an employee of Goth Enactments, I am not, so it would be right and proper if I explain what it is I do, chapter and verse." Bob, using the keys given to Luke by Pinko, unlocked all the necessary doors for them to make a full inspection. Frank, Sidney and the two girls could now simply walk in, when the time was right and straight down to the tunnel.

Sidney thought it an easy task, but the atmosphere generated by Mary was not conducive to coherent, lucid thought. It was obvious what needed to be done, but she was making it complicated by deep discussions about matters unrelated. She was obviously nervous, and Sidney ignored her, they were all following Frank's lead in any event, including Mary.

The war machine had no windows, so Sidney guessed Bob's assistant, Luke, would have no temptation to look down. The sun was setting, and dusk would be about ten thirty p.m. then darkness. They moved as silently as shadows; the reception area was pitch black. Frank waited until they were all in the storage room and the door closed before putting on the light. Sidney unbolted and pulled up the heavy sheet metal flap to the shaft and secured it with a steel chain and hook.

It was as Bob had described, the stair was now fully lit. Frank went down first, followed by Mary, then Penelope and Sidney following behind. They gathered at the bottom, Sidney was nervous and knew the other must be also. The opening was crudely formed, and the massively thick, ancient stone wall looked precarious overhead. "I will go in first," said Frank. "Not superiority I can assure you, just being cautious."

They followed him; in the same order they came down. They stood clustered together silently, in the dimly lit stone arched tunnel, the silence was one of unbelief at what they were looking at.

The five-metre-wide tunnel was dimly lit with temporary lighting, but what it revealed left them speechless. It was full of ancient Roman chariots, shields, helmets and countless other implements of war. "These are gladiator's weapons," said Mary. "All these are early Roman, this is incredible, how they have survived is a miracle." Sidney could see, as well as the poor lighting would allow, that in both directions along the tunnel, it was full of ancient armoury. It was clear that time had taken its toll and some of the wooden elements had long since rotted away, but the bronze and steel wheels, weapons and armour were in reasonably good condition.

"It is clear to me," said Mary. "that all this has been entombed for some reason, maybe for safekeeping, this is at least seventeen hundred years old." Sidney felt nervous again, this was all wrong, they shouldn't be here. He noticed, with relief, that none of the artefacts appeared to have been touched. Why he should feel so possessive he didn't know, but this find must be of national importance.

It was difficult to grasp the magnitude of it, but the geo-scans showed the tunnel to be about sixty metres long and the war machine was positioned in the middle. Sixty metres, over one hundred and eighty feet of priceless artefacts, a fragment of time that should belong to the nation.

"This is amazing." It was Penelope, she drew close to him. "What we are doing must be recorded." Her voice hushed. "This is too special to be treated casually." Sidney, like the rest of them, was mesmerised.

"Why are these people keeping this a secret and leaving it here untouched?" he said. "It doesn't make sense; the stair down here is for reason."

At that moment the lights went out and they were in complete darkness. In the silence and the blackness, the smell of age became pungent and claustrophobic; nobody spoke—it was the shock.

Frank switched on his torch and with some fumbling they all followed suit. It was then that the sound of the steel trap hatch above could be heard as it slammed shut, the sound echoing in the confined space was frightening; then the sharp cracks of the bolts being rammed into place; the final sound of their entrapment.

"Oh dear." Mary whispered.

"Wait here and I will go up and check." Sidney hoped he sounded confident. "Probably a simple mistake." They shouldn't be down here, he thought, so hardly likely. He climbed the stairs, his torch leading the way, it was easy to see and when he was only halfway up, he could see the steel hatch was firmly shut. He returned down to the others.

"I have been thinking." Frank was standing at the opening in the side of the tunnel. "The vaults we found are to the left along the tunnel about thirty metres, we know they are just behind a wall. Mary said there is a Roman structure there, perhaps they are connected; we may find a way through, a doorway perhaps, worth a try."

Sidney found it a difficult thirty metres; the main obstacles were the sharp and ragged steel spikes that protruded from the chariot wheel hubs. They climbed over various ancient weapons and steel-clad boxes with treasures hidden within, thought Sidney. They were careful not to disturb anything, the flashing of all their mobile phones was oddly comforting, twenty first century technology had come for a visit.

Sidney's sense of foreboding increased as they neared the end of the tunnel. There was no door, but it was obvious that the wall was later than the tunnel. And to Sidney's relief there was a high-level grill, just like the tunnel from the vaulting to the Castle dungeon. However, this did not quell his feeling of unease. He forced himself to be optimistic. "Well," he said, "This is encouraging, if we could pull a bar or two out, we may be able to climb through into the vaults we discovered and get out through the basement of Herbie's new house."

With this promise of hopeful safety, they eagerly searched

with their torches for something to lever with and something to stand on. Sidney hated doing this, for whatever they used was bound to have historic value but needs must be met. They used a heavy gladiator three-pronged trident, there were a whole collection, with shields, leaning against the stone wall of the tunnel.

Sidney was tallest; so, finding a suitable steel strapped chest to stand on he attacked two of the bars. Then stabbing and thrusting repeatedly for ten minutes at one bar, success, it came away. He repeated the exercise on the other one. He was starting to feel giddy now, the motionless air seemed to lack oxygen; he got down off the box breathing heavily.

Mary giggled nervously; there was hope now, albeit an escape from one basement into another. Sidney inspected the, all metal gladiator's trident, it looked well used now, but then after seventeen centuries one shouldn't be surprised, but he still felt guilty.

"I will go first," said Frank. "I will need to go through head and shoulders first, it may be difficult the other side, we will see. I can then help you down when you all pop through headfirst." Sidney thought the plan was sensible and they were all keen to escape; he pushed aside any negative thoughts of the murders and the possibility of them all starving to death.

CHAPTER 65
VISITORS

Bob was with Luke on the top floor of the war machine, and the view was something to talk about, they were discussing the surrounding area below, Bob had a plan of it. Then, they were both startled by the appearance of three men, they had made no sound when mounting the stairs. Bob knew immediately there could be trouble; he sensed that they had moved as though they were armed. He was armed himself and was immediately alert and looking for signs.

They were tough looking, and Bob reckoned them to be professional heavies. One of them, the biggest and first, looked contemptuously at Bob's security uniform. Bob just gave him a disarming grin and said, "Can I help you gentlemen?" it was nearly midnight, an ungodly hour one might say for a visit. The man stared at him, assessing him, did Bob pose a threat? Bob could see he wasn't sure.

Bob had been told in the past, that he did have an innocent way of looking that belied his real physical capabilities. To the three unexpected visitors he appeared to inexperienced in the ways of violence, a man who would be a weak link in a pathetic chain of command and of no consequence. He could read this in their faces.

Bob's mind was racing, fight or flight, what about the others down in the tunnel? He would need to warn them, he could feel his mobile buzzing in his pocket, it was on mute, he wondered who it was? He would need to be careful with these three.

"May I ask who you are?" said Luke, following Bob's lead.

"We work for Mr Jose, like you," said the big one. "We have come to protect you, matters have now escalated, Mr Jose is concerned for you, he doesn't want any more murders. We will be taking over security now, not your jobs, just the bigger picture; from now on you report to me." He handed Bob his mobile number on a piece of paper.

The man was not friendly, just menacing, Bob decided to carry on his eager to please act. "Escalated," he said, "You're getting busy then, we are as well, Luke here started only yesterday." He knew that was not what they meant, but he wanted their conversation to be kept as light as possible. If they had an inkling of what he was capable of, it would change everything.

"We wanted to come and see a professional security man in action." The sneer on the second man's face was ill-concealed. Bob was starting to be annoyed but kept tight lipped and mustered up another grin. One thing he was certain of, these were the enemy and sent by Jose. Luke was obviously Pinko's idea and ineffectual. He instinctively decided that he needed to protect Luke.

"I have to say, all the murders that took place were in the daytime; arrows flying all over the place, one man got a bolt through his chest just up there." He pointed to the small platform above. "But it's all quiet now, so not to worry." He could tell he was of no real interest to them, one of them was looking bored and hovering near the stair, obviously wanting to go. The big one looked intently at Bob and said, "Did you have any visitors in the night?" Bob looked at Luke. "No, we have been together all the time and we haven't met a soul."

The man wasn't going to give up that easily. "All the doors were open on the ground floor, is that usual?" Bob needed to pick he words carefully. "I usually open up, easier to inspect that way and with the flood lighting outside and cameras as a deterrent, I have never had any problems." He didn't bother to mention that he could switch them off. "As Mr Jose sent you?" his voice subservient. "Do you want me to keep you informed?" Bob waited as they moved towards the head to the stair, the big man turned.

"No," he replied, "I will contact you if I need anything, I've got your number."

They were left alone. "Gosh," Luke blurted out. "They were a strange bunch, did you see the big one's hands, like a gorilla's only wider."

CHAPTER 66

Frank called Bob again, he answered this time. "Sorry Frank, we have had visitors and not particularly friendly ones, they have just gone so we can talk." Frank listened while he gave him the update. "Ok Bob, well you have no need to open up the tunnel, we have found a way out. There is access to adjoining vaults, the ones at the back of Castle Ditch House, Herbie's place. We are there now, that's why I got a phone connection. I think Herbie's the only one that can let us out, unless we break out; our torches are getting dim."

He listened to Bob's response and relayed it to the others. "Bob's going to unlock the doors for us, one of his talents. He will be here in a few minutes," he said, "Apparently he has had visitors, looks like the enemy has been alerted and Bob says not to involve Herbie, he doesn't trust him."

Sidney was wondering how the girls were faring, he felt emotionally and physically exhausted. The energy he had expended on the iron bars had left him groggy, it was too much effort in too short a time and driven by fear for the safety of the girls. This creeping around, in the middle of the night and trapped in a place they should not be and unable to communicate with anyone, was not conducive to a relaxed evening.

It was a relief when Frank contacted Bob, at the other end of the tunnel there was no reception, they had all tried. All they had to do now was wait for Bob to let them out.

Mary's inquisitive nature was helpful, taking their minds off their circumstances. "I suggest we have a tour of the vaults," she said, "while we wait, I haven't seen all of it; the lighting was distracting before; having just our torches we can focus better as we move along, and I want to show you the Roman part of the under-croft." They followed her along the perimeter, which to Sidney's surprise started to curve and so did the column lines, he had not noticed that before.

They then came to the discovered tunnel that they thought was a tunnel built by attackers of the castle. "No this is Roman," Mary said, "and is a tunnel leading, not out to the west, but into this vaulted underground part of an amphitheatre. Like the tunnel we have just come through from the opposite direction, the east. The curved section we have just seen is a fragment of the huge circular structure. "The enthusiasm in her voice was infectious.

"So, the construction of Battle-Cry Castle is a relatively recent innovation in the scheme of things," said Sidney. "I find it difficult to take that in—1066 and all that, it's like missing a thousand years."

At that, the lights when on. "Oh, what a relief," Mary said. "That will be Bob." There was a rattling of keys in the distance, they made their way to the ramped tunnel entrance.

Bob opened the door before they got there, his face was beaming. "Am I glad to see you, my mighty warriors." He laughed; it was a nervous one; he quickly gave Mary a hug.

CHAPTER 67
BLIND PANIC

Pinko had been summoned to see Chief Exec Jose. He knew it was serious, the tone of his voice said as much, but then the whole business was serious, things were getting out of hand. "Progress is too slow," he had growled on the phone. "Be here tomorrow morning at ten o'clock sharp."

On the train to London, he had time to reflect on the current dire situation and how he could improve on it. The very thing he had been hired to hide and protect had become vulnerable. It was the timing; they should have taken the Roman treasure trove weeks ago, as he had suggested. The irritating thing was Jose's controlling behaviour, he had to be right in everything and it was this that had caused the present crisis, for which he would be blamed not Jose. But then, he was the boss and knew everything.

It was fine at the beginning, he had full control of the ramp construction and the digging out of the shaft; the whole thing took eight weeks with no hold ups. Since then, Jose's constant interference has caused no end of problems. His constant monitoring and irrational decisions were causing confusion and discord among the three men employed as so-called operators but were really brought in as labour to move the treasure. He had enough problems without adding to them by criticising his boss, the instigator of them. He got a taxi to Bryanston Square with a heavy heart.

"Come in, come in," said Jose, his face showed no emotion as usual. His plush office had the aroma of freshly made coffee. Jose gestured to a chair in front of his huge desk, which seemed to Pinko to be more like an ornate counter in a hardware shop than a plush office desk; he waited.

"Now Pinko, I have to tell you I am getting more annoyed by the day; if we do not take action and remove all the Roman artefacts from the tunnel soon, our arrangement with the Russian dealer will fall through." He paused, his face mottled and quivering with anger. "We have left it too long already, the whole collection was photographed and left untouched, just as he wanted; to delay anymore is too risky."

Pinko was past caring. His boss was using the words like, we, and our, as though Pinko was part of a team. There was no team only Jose, who though he had total autonomy wanted to appear blameless.

"And another thing," continued Jose, "this Norman Keep you employed, he made a good job of distracting and a good job of disappearing, where is he? Fat lot of good he is." His face was puffed and red with indignation, he didn't wait for Pinko to answer, which was a relief to Pinko as he didn't have one. "And the hot air balloon saga, don't tell me that was Norman Keep's fault, is that why he's run away? Cowards the lot of them." He made no mention of the death and destruction that was left in the wake of Norman Keep's efforts to gain a distraction, on his orders.

He glared at Pinko, daring him to answer, he did. "I think we should be cautious Jose." His use of Alfonso Jose's surname was a mark of respect; he knew Jose liked it. "I have put in a new man to monitor Bob from the security company, to be on the safe side."

"Yes, I got your memo, well that's not good enough, I have now put the overall responsibility for security into the hands of Karl and his two cousins." Pinko remembered them from the Midlands job, they were a nasty piece of work, thugs; things could get worse; his heart sank. "Oh yes and another thing, that Bob on security is sloppy. According to Karl, the trap hatch to the tunnel was left unlocked, this is not good enough Pinko, deal with the man, or I will. I need more time, not more stress."

Pinko came away from the meeting suitably chastised and none the wiser. When would the treasure be moved? Only time would tell. He realised that every day that passed increased the risk that the tunnel would be found and what then? The treasure would be lost. Goth Enactments had invested a lot of money and were greedy for a return, there were two men higher than Jose and all would not be well for any of them if they were disappointed.

He tried to think on the positive side as he travelled back. This was a fantastic find and must remain a secret until the deal was done, he could only guess why the delay, it must be to do with money. He had created as many distractions as he could, including the seed sown that the war machine arm was some sort of secret weapon, when it was the building inspector that wanted the swing arm completed, for health and safety reasons.

Pinko's feeling was, that Jose was leaving things too late. Goth Enactments were basically stealing, robbing the British nation's treasures and there was a stronger possibility now that they would be caught. The Russian buyer must make a move soon, otherwise he would need to disappear himself; he did have a contingency plan.

CHAPTER 68
STALEMATE

Pinko decided to give Luke a serious briefing, his induction had been a bit casual, but he was concerned about Bob. He seemed a nice enough chap, but he suspected, inquisitive. He mustn't be allowed to discover the tunnel, that would be disastrous.

"We need to have a strict routine for the two of you Luke." They had met in his office after Luke's second night.

"That's easier said than done," he replied. "He's already arranged it and shown it to me, it seems OK. He seems a sensible guy to work with; he got on well with the three men sent by Mr Jose, but I will keep my eye on him."

Pinko was relieved when he mentioned the three visitors and Bob's reaction, his doubts about Bob were fading. "That's fine, but please note anything unusual, we have big Karl and his cousins on the case now and you can rely on them, they are experienced operators." He was aware that Luke was not, but he would have preferred him than them, they were more than a little wayward.

Pinko had prepared a plan for removing the Roman artefacts two months ago, but Jose had chosen to ignore it, which was his way of refusing to accept it. Jose had a massive control problem: Pinko had experienced this with him on the Midlands project, but not as serious as this. Because Jose was approving someone else's idea or work, he would perceive that as losing control in some way, and that to him was unacceptable.

Pinko felt sure that if the two major investors and directors above Jose knew what he was doing, or to be precise, not doing, they would be mortified, there was so much at stake. Pinko had realised that Jose was taking the same stance with the Russian dealers, they wanted something and were prepared to pay for it, but it was subject to demands. Jose saw these demands as being told what to do and so he did nothing; it had been stalemate for the past eight weeks.

Pinko, though having criminal tendencies, was reasonably straight forward in his dealings. Consequently, he was at a loss to understand Jose and was now formulating his own plan. It would be a miracle if the deal worked out and as he had never experienced a miracle, he had little hope.

Pinko was a tough character, but totally shocked by Norman Keep's killing spree. He was keeping his head down on that one, he didn't want to be joining them in the morgue. It was obviously Jose's doing and an irrational act of misplaced power. His course of action was obvious now: he must get out and as quickly as possible.

The three Russian workers were employed by the Russian dealer and could only be relied upon to do their masters bidding, and so everybody was waiting for Jose's instructions. And that is what Jose liked, the power, but misused power could prove to be costly.

CHAPTER 69
CONFLICT

The atmosphere of their usual morning meeting was tense. They were all tired from lack of sleep, but Frank was insistent. "We meet while things are still fresh in our minds, its hard but best." They all had some time to reflect on the night's dramatic happenings and the discovery of a hidden tunnel that was being kept secret. But what was truly amazing were the remains of a Roman Amphitheatre, hidden for all those years under the feet of the residents of Cry City.

There was no doubt that what they had witnessed was world-wide news. Words were inadequate to express the level of importance of this find and its impact on English history. Sidney could see that Frank was endeavouring to marshal the troops—Mary, Penelope, himself and Bob. Frank was quiet and respectful, clearly wanting to put them at ease, they settled and waited for him to continue.

"I want you to know," he said earnestly, "that you will not be alone, I have arranged for a squad of SAS soldiers to monitor the whole site. Sadly, we cannot trust the local police force now. I have given them photographs of all four of you for recognition, you will not know they are there." Frank stopped for a moment looking for a reaction, they said nothing, he continued.

"They have been given instructions from high up in Whitehall, who are aware that plans are being made to steal the Roman artefacts. Any attempts to move anything will be robustly dealt with and the men will swoop and secure it. One might say it is secure already, but the top commander wants to catch them in the act. Otherwise, Goth Enactments could counter claim for damages and that really wouldn't do."

He sat on the edge of his chair. "Three murders have taken place and justice must be done." He paused looking intently at the three, Bob was standing aside. "You three are not combatants and Bob and I are responsible for you; you have all done very well so far and thank you for that, but now it goes up a gear and a certain level of experience is needed in dealing with miscreants of this calibre. There will be physical danger, of that I am sure, so I would ask, that you two wait for our instructions."

Sidney was pleased for Penelope and Mary they would be out of danger, whatever that danger might be, but if Norman Keep is anything to go by, it could be serious, and Jose should not be underestimated. Frank continued, "Actually Sidney, we want you to carry on as normal, if you don't mind, we don't want Pinko getting wind of what we are up to."

Sidney was happy with the outcome, more so for Mary and Penelope, he would prefer that they were as far away as possible. Frank then addressed something that was in the back of everyone's mind.

"I mentioned to you all a while ago that I was concerned about Herbert Strange. Well, we have him in custody now and I am unhappy with his explanation regarding the purchase of Castle Ditch House. We all know that from the vaults, access is possible to link all the tunnels, and this means Mr Strange potentially, if not actually, has access to them all. All this is too much of a coincidence I am afraid; we need to stop him communicating." Sidney felt sorry for Herbie, he lived alone and was on the eccentric side and it was so easy to misinterpret his actions, so he thought it a wise decision to put him in custody, if only for his own safety. He felt sure there was a simple explanation.

CHAPTER 70
CONTROL

Jose had not briefed Karl and his two cousins adequately, his theory was, if he told them too much it would reduce his control over them and at the same time increase theirs. As he was engaged in all these mental gymnastics, he was unwittingly losing control. Pinko could see all this; he had a few years of first-hand experience dealing with Jose's idiosyncrasies, but sadly, powerless to do anything about it. His personal focus now, was on a graceful, non-profitable exit alive.

Pinko felt uneasy, this state of limbo was not in the plan, the Roman treasure was there for the taking so why not take it? Jose's reticence to divulge his plans was infuriating but wait he must. His survival instinct was telling him that Sidney could be a useful ally if things got difficult. Their offices were adjoining, so communication was not difficult. He could see that Sidney was surprised when he suggested they have lunch together, which was to be expected, considering it would be the first time after working together for six months.

The morning went slowly and Pinko was pleased when lunch time came. They made their way to the Italian restaurant in the High Street. The food was ordered, and they sat waiting with a glass of wine. "Have you enjoyed working on the project Sidney?" His question was simple enough, but not considering that Jose and himself had made things difficult for

Sidney on many occasions, well more Jose than himself. Nevertheless, Sidney had been constantly side-lined, and he was therefore surprised at his graceful reply.

"Well, Pinko, I must say it has been a privilege to work on a project of this of this magnitude. The scale model alone, was a project and so yes, I have enjoyed it, with all the sling arm's ups and downs."

Pinko laughed, he couldn't help it, he warmed to Sidney and felt guilty about the veil of secrecy he had put up. It would have been much better if he could have been far more open, but Jose forbade it. The project had been introduced by DI Buck, and that's why he had to go with him and Jasper Thorndyke, who was in on it. Their roles were minor, but connections that Jose wanted to cut off, and the way things were going himself as well, nothing was certain with Jose in charge.

They finished the meal and Pinko had enjoyed Sidney's company. "I do hope everything works out for you Sidney life has a funny way of turning things on their head. I am hopeful to move on myself soon." They sauntered back to the office, talking about structural oak. Their bond was the war machine, with all its design and logistical construction challenges. Pinko felt annoyed, he had lost the opportunity for a lasting friendship with Sidney. The desire for money and power had been too strong. It was too late now, there could be only one outcome.

CHAPTER 71
KARL

Karl was a man of action, whether it was positive action or badly timed action, it was all the same to him. 'Actions speak louder than words', his favourite motto. The fact that Mr Jose had not been clear when he gave him instructions, did not take away the fact that Jose needed action, and action he would get. The situation needed a stirring up, and he had a plan, he would target Bob the security man, the one with the neat uniform.

The man irritated him, maybe it was his calm unruffled reaction to his attempt at intimidating him, he was too cocky for his own good. He would give him a shock, Ken and Jack his cousins were up for it, they would pay friend Bob a visit.

They arrived on site at fifteen minutes to midnight. They found Bob in Sidney's office with Luke, they had just finished their first tour of duty. "Just the man we want to see; we like a man in uniform, don't we boys." He sniggered; his two boys followed suit. Bob stood facing them; Luke was sitting staring.

"What do you want to see me about?" Bob's voice was calm, firm, that annoyed Karl.

"Get that jacket off and I'll show you." He leered, smug in the knowledge of his power, he was six feet two and knew it. What happened next, he never did quite remember, it was too fast. Bob casually walked towards them and moved as though he was about to take off his jacket. Instead of that, he kicked out viciously and connected with Karl's left knee cap.

Then almost in the same movement and as Karl staggered back in agony, his second kick with his left foot found the ankle of the man on Karl's right, he yelped and skipped back. The third man stood frozen, he was standing behind them and couldn't do anything anyway.

It wasn't silent, there was heavy breathing and groaning, but Bob wasn't finished. "I will give you some advice, which I suggest you take heed of, never, ever threaten or intimidate a security guard, you are liable to get yourself hurt. Now I suggest you get out before I throw you out." He stood calmly looking at them, obviously waiting for them to go.

Karl was standing, bent slightly and nursing his knee cap. The other helper sat down nursing his ankle, which was placed on the knee of his opposite leg, his cursing was colourful. Bob had successfully immobilised two, at least for a few minutes, the third had no fight in him, he was waiting for instructions from Karl.

This man is quick, thought Karl, gritting his teeth in fury and pain. He had seriously underestimated him, he decided that revenge would be sweeter later, but then they would be armed. His exit did not have the same impact as his entrance as he was limping and felt like a drink.

CHAPTER 72
PRESSURE.

Jose was under increasing pressure from the Russians, they had agreed a deal, paid the procurement deposit and expected delivery of the Roman treasure. It was one million down payment, which was in a joint account and the full twenty million would be paid when their men had the artefacts. Their men were on site and had arranged transport, it would need to be a speedy and secret operation. It was a massive deal and all those involved were getting anxious.

However, there was a problem, and the problem was Jose. He suffered from a narcissistic personality and lacked empathy with his business associates, or anyone else for that matter. His grandiose sense of self-importance ruled his decision making and being always right in his own eyes. This would often mean he would make no decision, just to be on the safe side, as in the present case. A criminal's opportunity of a lifetime held up by a personality disorder, but then is a criminal normal?

The Russians had started off with reasonable requests, which Jose regarded as telling him what to do, and nagging, so he ignored them. These requests then turned into demands, which Jose also ignored as he regarded these as, once again telling him what to do. He had a sense of peace about it because he believed he was always right; in fact, he was convinced of it.

He preferred to stay in London and let Pinko carry out his

instructions, that way he could avoid blame in the event of a failed mission. Jose would never admit it, but he was a coward hiding behind a thin veneer of bluster and intermittent swear words and to a certain extent the cleverness of a criminal mind.

Apart from the Russians, Jose was now under pressure from his two bosses, the major shareholders and senior directors. They had told him in no uncertain terms that the Russians should take the Roman treasure and give them the twenty million pounds sterling. Sadly, because Jose could not be told what to do, he took no action. Employing Karl and his cousins was his way of moving forward in a manner that would not bring a railing judgement from his superiors, though he refused to see them as that, which was the root of his problem. Narcissism was a difficult condition to live with, for him and all those around him, he was of course blissfully unaware of it.

The only person who really understood him was Pinko, good faithful Pinko, ever ready to help and in all things uncomplaining, he hated people who complained. His only hope now was Karl and his cousins, he had no idea what they would do, but if it was a big enough fuss, he could hide behind that and it would give him more time to make a decision. At all costs he must avoid being told what to do.

CHAPTER 73
THE MOVE

Vilius had run out of patience. "This idiot Alfonso Jose will ruin the deal if we don't act immediately." He was addressing his Russian men, hand-picked to move the Roman artefacts. They were three of the best, tough resilient and military trained. They were also unimpressed by Goth Enactments' lack lustre approach to the moving arrangement. It would take at least a month to move it all, if not more and Jose had lost them three months by his pontificating.

"I have decided that we start moving the Roman treasure tomorrow night. All small items, that is pieces that can be picked up and carried in two hands by one person, shall be carried to the reception area and numbered, photographed and boxed. The laser survey plan you did, I suggest you mark up a copy showing the position of the items, as found. The most important thing is to keep our private collector happy; I know we have gone through all this before, but his curator is a stickler for protocol and will be making sure the goods get to the warehouse safely. We must also remind ourselves of the prize, our share, twenty million English pounds is a lot of money. All this activity should not attract attention, I have organised two large, transit type vans."

The men were smiling, relieved that there was action at last, Vilius continued. "I reckon it will take about two weeks plus, to move all the smaller items from out of the tunnel, this will make room to get to the bigger ones. We may have to store some in the war machine on the levels above, I know that was what we originally intended, but we need to move fast now and get them on the road."

One of the men wanted to know when they could work in the daytime. "I would suggest you work in shifts to suit yourselves, but I can get extra drivers for shifting the stuff. We need to be careful, that's all. The seven chariots will be last, they will need careful dismantling, they are mainly bronze and the prize items." His voice expressed his keenness to get things going. "We will need to inform Bob the security man and his assistant, we have no choice as he works nights. We may also encounter Pinko, I will deal with them, when they challenge us. But it is important we say nothing of our plans until the moment we start. We need to control the site, the war machine and the tunnel, Jose's complete lack of respect will not be tolerated anymore."

CHAPTER 74
VILIUS

Karl in his quest for action, had picked the same night to make his non-friendly visit to Bob, as Vilius had for taking over the site, and the war machine. Both were acts of aggression and any clash would bring about violent results. Each agenda that Karl and Vilius had, stemmed from Jose's reticence to commit himself.

Karl arrived on site at ten p.m. it was nearly dark, and he used his keys to open the perimeter gate. He was hoping to catch Bob in Sidney's office, but he wasn't there. He decided to set off towards the war machine, the next obvious place. There were no windows, but he could see glimpses of light coming from under the entrance door, he released the strap over the holster of his gun. With his cousins close behind he opened and pushed the door inwards and walked in. Vilius's men were busy in the reception area filling numerous boxes of varying sizes on the floor with old implements of some sort.

They looked up, Karl could tell that they were up to no good, their look was hard and wary. He walked confidently towards them, they did not move or acknowledge him; he knew his boys were close behind. "What do you think you're up to?" His voice hard and commanding, there was a silence. "Well, who gave you permission to do this?" He had no proof that they were doing anything illegal, it was pure instinct, but his instinct he could trust. He was armed and so were his boys.

He waited; the taller one answered.

"Sorry, were you not informed? We are getting ready to move some artefacts for storage, Vilius our boss arranged it, we are working late to meet a deadline." Karl was suspicious, he was always suspicious of foreigners out of principal. This man's voice sounded eastern European, the accent could be Russian.

"Can I see proof of your identity?" Karl was trying to be patient; the man's reply didn't help.

"We work here, Bob the security guard has our details."

This sounded reasonable, but Karl wasn't happy, working at night seemed a bit strange; conservation work was normally a daytime activity. He went on another tack. "Where has all this stuff come from?" This question seemed to catch the man off guard, Karl could sense he didn't want to answer, so he pressed him again. "What part of the site did this come from?"

As he asked the question, he was conscious that he had not introduced himself, they had no idea that he and his cousins worked for Jose as extra security. He wondered why they hadn't asked, his unease grew. The man answered abruptly. "It came from the tunnel, that's all." The tone of his voice told Karl that this was going to be heavy weather.

He responded in a like manner. "Oh, and where is this tunnel?" It was Karl's question that changed everything.

The tall man turned to his comrades and spoke in his native tongue; they all immediately moved closer together and towards Karl and the boys and they did not look friendly. Karl was just about to pull his gun out when Bob and his sidekick Luke came down the stairs.

Bob's first thoughts were, as he looked at the scene before him, what a bizarre situation for the middle of the night. Three

Russians taking treasure illegally, three criminals employed by Jose to cause mischief and to protect treasure that they didn't even know existed. And now himself, a trained SAS officer. And then there was Luke—a callow youthful overseer not long out of school and with no idea of the seriousness of it all.

"Don't let us interrupt you gentlemen," said Bob. "Luke and I are going walkabout, should be back in about an hour." He made his way quickly to the exit door followed by Luke and they left. Frank's orders had been quite specific when they had spoken on their mobiles. "Do not get into confrontations, I know what you are like, we must catch them in the act."

Bob needed to get Luke out of the way; he had not challenged the Russians when he first met them on his inspection earlier crating up the artefacts, he took their reasons for working late as gospel, as Frank wanted. He was surprised that they were moving the artefacts tonight, it was a bit sudden. When he phoned Frank and informed him of events. "OK, Bob, it looks like tonight is the night, we mustn't allow anything to be removed from site. Whitehall will have me roasted if anything is lost, this is of national importance. And please keep Luke away from the action, we can't afford to have casualties, we have had enough already."

Things were more complicated now with the arrival of this character Karl and his accomplices, they had been sent by Jose, but what had he instructed them to do? Bob decided to leave the problem with the SAS men and concentrate on looking after Luke. He turned on all the site floodlighting, knowing there were seven men looking after them, he then explained the situation to Luke, if anything went wrong, he would need to take instructions immediately. He took it well and was eager to help.

CHAPTER 75
THE BUST

Frank was getting slightly stressed now, he had put the SAS team of seven on full alert and instructed them to move in slowly and keep hidden. Bob had told him he was now away from the war machine and in the site office with Luke. Frank was with the SAS Commander Kemp, they were in a white van close to the site, and from the windows had a clear view of the site, which was bathed in light.

"This has been a long-time coming, Frank." Dan Kemp had been on standby for three weeks ready for the go—he, Frank and Bob were part of a strong team. Frank was his superior officer and Bob under his joint command with Frank. "I have told Bob to hold back." Frank said. "He's on site, but he tells me he's in Sidney's office and he's floodlit the whole site to help us."

The surveillance van had two periscopes mounted on the roof—two operatives could maintain a constant three-hundred-and-sixty-degree panoramic view, if need be. It could extend up another two metres above the roof. The body of the van was bulletproof.

Frank's mobile buzzed—it was Bob. "Hi, Frank, I'm sending out Luke, I have told him to casually go outside the perimeter fence as though inspecting, and when he has passed the point of being visible from the war machine, can you pick him up? We will not get another chance; it could get nasty here." Frank was relieved, another risk factor removed.

Dan had given the keys to Castle Ditch House to a corporal, he and two others were down in the vaults waiting at the end of the tunnel. They had stationed themselves by the grill that Sidney had forced open. If there was an attempt made to get out there, the Russians would be caught. All precautions had been made and everyone was in place for the planned offensive, which was agreed at fourteen hundred hours.

Then something strange happened, Pinko phoned Bob on his mobile and what he had to say made them wait. Bob had recorded Pinko's message then downloaded it and sent it on to Frank. It was short, to the point, and surprising.

"I have arranged for Alfonso Jose to be at the war machine in one hour, he is under the impression that Vilius is desperate, I have told him that Vilius will do anything to get things moving and could Jose meet him at the war machine, Vilius would pay handsomely. Jose is coming because he thinks he is in control and won, he thinks I will be there also, but that will not be the case. Of course, I know the site is under surveillance I have known that for two weeks now. I suggest you can now arrest Jose and the others for stealing the nation's treasures.

I am disappearing with no financial gain and also Pinko is not my real name, so you will not be able to find me, I hope justice will be done and for the record, I had nothing to do with the deaths, that was Alfonso Jose's doing. I have left proof of this in my office it shouldn't be that hard to find." That was the message, it was cutting it fine, but it was obvious that Pinko had picked his timing carefully, no doubt engineered to make his escape when the focus was on catching the others.

"All we have to do now is wait," said Frank, "and catch Jose and the Russian dealers handling the treasure."

Karl was still in the war machine having a stand-off with the Russians when Jose arrived, he had driven from London setting off just after midnight, he was not best pleased. Bob had greeted him at the site office, he had left the gate open for him to drive in. He took Jose to the war machine, opened the entrance door for him to go in and closing it after him carefully, then went back to his office.

The following course of events was gleaned from the seven miscreants disjointed accounts, as noted in the police reports, but furnished by the SAS.

When Alfonso Jose appeared, casually walking through the entrance door of the war machine at two in the morning, it was a shock to them all. He looked around. "Where is Vilius?" he frowned, then scowled. "I am to meet him here." He saw Karl. "What are you doing here?" Karl was incensed and reddened with anger, being spoken to like that was bad enough, but in front of these Russians and his cousins. that was just too much. It was at that moment that he realised that Jose regarded him as just a smear of mud on his shoe; he let his anger run full reign.

Karl moved forward quickly and surprised everyone, not least Alfonso Jose, who received one of Karl's massive fists full in the face. The impact was audible and the groan that followed was more of a sob. Karl turned and snarled to his boys that they should leave. He went to the door and yanked the handle, it did not yield, Bob had locked it from the outside. The door was too heavy to get physical with and so he kicked it instead.

His reaction to this indignity was kick it again and roar. "Damn and blast it." Jose was sitting down, nursing his damaged face in his hands, he looked up, his normally red bloated features had taken on a bluish tinge. The Russians looked panicky and decided to go to the top of the war machine from the inside and scale down the outside. They spoke in Russian, so nobody knew of their intention; armed SAS troops were at the bottom and caught them with aggressive enthusiasm.

Alfonso Jose was left with a belligerent Karl standing, towering over him. He had no chance of escape; his weight was against flight and he couldn't fight. His world of power and control was about to evaporate, as though it had never been.

Not a shot was fired, or physical violence used, putting aside the damage to Jose's nose. The armed SAS eagerly grappled with the descending Russians as the abseiled down the outside of the war machine. They were not treated kindly; the safety of the nation's treasure was at stake and the frustration of waiting had shown itself in the violent way they dealt with the Russians, who would be nursing bruises for weeks.

Alfonso Jose's robust stature seemed to have shrunk, as they led him away. Karl and his boys were destined for a night in prison. The SAS were taking no chances, if someone came across as a hard man, treat him as such, his boys were treated the same. They were totally innocent of any wrongdoing, Jose's nose aside, they were just at the wrong place at the wrong time and with the wrong attitude. The only positive thing that stood Karl in good stead was his street cred. He was known from then on as the man on the inside of the bust.

CHAPTER 76
FUTURE

It became obvious as time went on and legal investigations took place, that Pinko, or whatever his name was, had added stipulations to the legal documentation and this was executed by the lawyers and was binding. It stated that in the event of Goth Enactments failing to meet its commitments or the company being liquidated, the ownership of the war machine would be signed over to Sidney Picket. The designer and builder. This documentation was completed only two weeks ago and clearly part of Pinko's own exit plan.

Sidney felt sorry that he had not been more charitable towards him, but he was a criminal, albeit likeable. He was a character, of that there was no doubt and Sidney hoped they would meet up again one day.

Now Sidney was the proud owner of a war machine of worldwide fame. He and Penelope had decided that they would only throw balloons at it, at Christmas times. It would also remain static and be used as a permanent entrance to the tunnel for the public to view the Roman chariots, artefacts and the underground amphitheatre vaulting. The gate fee takings were beyond all expectations.

It was a great success and became a World Heritage site, visited by academics from all over the globe. Bob and Mary got married and travelled with his unit. Penelope said she would marry him, and they had fixed a date.

It was a strange thing, but the impact of the whole experience had left Sidney with a void in his life, he wanted to do it again, the desire for discovery that had now become an obsession. It was a yearning, an insatiable force that must be satisfied, but where should he go next?

THE END